TRAPPED BETWEEN TWO WORLDS: THE ANGEL WITHOUT WINGS

A Novel of Atlantis, Crete, and Ancient Egypt

MICHAEL RAY LEMONS

Book design and Cover design by Priya Paulraj

ISBN: 979-8-9885303-5-0

Printed in the United States of America

Acknowledgements

For all of you who believed in me and allowed my voice to touch your life, this novel proves that your love gave me the courage to take this leap of faith.

I truly appreciate all the prayers sent to the highest heavens to save me, granting me the ability to bless others during this spiritual journey. Gratefully, I acknowledge your inspiration and the strength you've given me to withstand my harshest critics.

I'm deeply grateful to my daughter, Haley, for reading the beginning of my manuscript and critiquing my writing style most mindfully and gently.

History is important, but so is imagination, which helps fill in gaps left by stories that leave us in unknown territory.

I'm gratified to write about characters in Atlantis, Crete, and Egypt with the seed of faith in a higher power that supersedes all our understanding. I loved every minute of researching this story.

So many have touched my life most profoundly without knowing they'd made a difference. Thank you for being a blessing to me and making my life better. For everything, a purpose challenges the narrative of life's journey.

And above all, I give thanks to my God, Yahweh, our beloved Creator, who carried me this distance with love, forgiveness, and the strength to make life changes possible.

*This book is dedicated to Austin and Laylani,
two of my grandkids who scribbled over the notes of this novel. I
appreciate the gesture of love and the precious memories, which serve as
a reminder that your mother, Haley,
had done the same for the rough draft of my first book,
Cush to Mysterious Babylon, more than twenty years earlier.*

Table of Contents

Introduction

THIS STORY BEGAN in the Mediterranean, where history comes alive, and the brilliance of sunshine dissolves into various shades of color before fading into twilight. The people of the Mediterranean lived in a distinct world of their own and with tolerance to achieve great things.

Before recorded history, families fled Africa by blindly sailing the blue ocean toward an undetermined destination. The adventure must have outweighed the risk, and their reward was a journey through turquoise water and the settling of wondrous islands scattered across the Aegean Sea. The waterway of the Mediterranean harbored permanent settlements on separate isles into the Aegean Sea.

The new settlers built flourishing cities and burgeoning ports and developed well-appointed governments with lavish royal palaces. The wonderful empires of Atlantis and Crete sat opposite the mouth of the Mediterranean Sea.

On the Aegean Islands, the Minoans of Crete produced the first urban civilization in Europe during the period of the Bronze Age. One could trace the emergence of the earliest Cretan civilizations to the large-scale migration from North Africa to the Aegean Islands to build the great cities of Atlantis and Crete.

The Minoans of Crete established great trade throughout the Mediterranean with lucrative commerce from cultivation and irrigation techniques. They also built one of the world's first sewage treatment and water purification systems. However, jealousy and envy turned the coast of the Mediterranean into a bloody warzone.

The ingenious Cretans were responsible for the first paved roads, masterfully supplying fresh water to homes and public spaces using hidden drainage systems. The highly intelligent Minoans, led by the most brilliant engineers, held power over the Mediterranean, expanding their maritime trade to locations such as the Aegean Islands, India, Egypt, Spain, and parts of Africa. This trade brought them incredible wealth and fostered strong financial connections between African nations and the Aegean Islands.

Unfortunately, a devastating volcanic eruption sent tidal waves crashing onto Crete's shores, ruining plantations, crops, and merchant vessels. This calamity devastated Crete's coastline and neighboring coastal towns; even 3,000 miles away one could hear the explosion's rumble. Overwhelmed by volcanic eruptions and earthquakes, most of the Cretan population struggled to recover, leading to the sudden disappearance of Europe's first great and powerful civilization.

A formidable king with the title Minos ruled over the Mediterranean maritime economy. The history of Atlantis and much of Crete became intertwined with classical Greek mythology. Mediterranean wealth circulated through Egyptian territory down to the Nile Delta, as Minoan trade thrived until it was disrupted by Indo-European conquerors from the Balkans.

In the south, the Cushites imported and exported large quantities of myrrh, incense, spice, gold, birds, animal skins, and meat from various animals. There was a market system that depended upon some long-distance caravans, and from coastal waters brought into the Nile Delta markets.

The Egyptians sailed down the coast of the Nile, bringing back commodities, ivory, and much-needed timber from the coastal cities of Africa. They traded with the Ethiopians and Nubians throughout the Aegean Islands, including Crete. The communication was adequate, with almost no separation before the Balkan invasion.

The Atlanteans were not only stunning but also possessed advanced technical abilities, similar to their Aegean Islander counterparts. Atlantis was a land brimming with blessings from the Creator, which seemed almost magical in nature. Their profound understanding of life's secrets, gifted them with exceptional cultivation skills and a deep-rooted spirituality that influenced the world around them.

Wherever the Atlanteans settled in the Aegean, the Creator's blessings and grace accompanied them. These divine favors granted the Islanders a fulfilling life as long as they upheld perfection in service and shunned the pagan gods from foreign lands.

Originating from Africa alongside the Minoans of Crete, the Atlanteans dispersed throughout the Mediterranean and across the islands of the Aegean.

Society may have forgotten about the past glory of Africa and the Mediterranean, but archaeologists have stirred up their histories from beneath the earth. The view of Atlantis had been twisted and turned inside and out—enough for evidence to float right up to the surface.

The Mediterranean is a unique ecosystem characterized by its lush woodlands, diverse vegetation, vibrant wildlife, and treasure trove of rare minerals. The Aegean Islands stretch across the Mediterranean, presenting a one-of-a-kind lifestyle centered around bustling harbors and bountiful resources.

In this fascinating region, ancient stories of prosperity are etched in pyramid walls adorned with vivid illustrations depicting daily life. Hieroglyphics on grand monuments reveal the thriving trade routes and commerce of a bygone era. The awe-inspiring art captures the essence of majestic rivers, dazzling skies, and the boundless imagination of this remarkable civilization. Papyrus paper served as the canvas for recording everyday business dealings.

Atlantis, Crete, and Egypt were magnificent utopias with astonishing architecture that easily rivaled the most impressive engineering marvels of antiquity. Boasting governments as advanced as those in modern societies, these places were truly ahead of their time.

The Atlanteans shared a deep connection with the Minoans of Crete—the two societies lived extravagantly in their respective twin cities. Gifted with exceptional engineering skills, abundant natural resources, and fertile agricultural lands, these three shining utopias set the stage for their own future triumphs.

Atlantis and its fellow empires were unique, with each great power exhibiting its dazzling style of engineering and architecture. They showcased their superior ingenuity with canals used to collect and store rain, which provided water throughout their metropolitan areas.

The Mediterranean world left a beacon of wisdom, featuring an intricate network of aqueducts, complex earthen levees, and agricultural and political structures.

They developed a flourishing economic system with ships and seaports and had a very high level of intelligence. The sea's horizon brought a flourishing economy and ensured remarkable prosperity that revolutionized the Mediterranean world.

There were no secrets, just a network of trade routes that paraded their way of life through the Nile. The Mediterranean world was paradise—an authentic Garden of Eden built by African people.

Imperial Atlantis designed its capital with a dazzling blend of rubies, sapphires, and sparkling white gemstones. Its structure was five zones in perfect concentric circles with luxurious baths and running water carried by aqueducts beneath the ground.

During the chilly winters, the homes in Atlantis stayed cozy, thanks to hot steam heating. These houses boasted water purification systems, bathtubs, and flushing toilets as standard features. The mythical land was nourished by mountain streams, which irrigated the fertile soil and ensured water access even in the most remote locations. Atlantis flourished with towns, palaces, and a strong military presence, shielding it from the bonds of tyranny.

The Atlanteans held dominion over several nearby islands and regions within Africa and Europe. However, their civilization ultimately fell victim to the volcanic eruption of Thera—today's Santorini near Crete in the Aegean Sea.

In this legendary city, laws were etched onto pillars made of orichalcum, an alloy composed of copper, nickel, and zinc. Over time, the people lost favor with the gods, leading to their tragic end as the blue waves of the Aegean Sea engulfed them at the Mediterranean's western edge.

The Creator's anger swelled as Atlanteans began to worship carved idols and honor foreign, pagan gods. Plunging into darkness fueled by desire, the Atlanteans could no longer protect themselves from the malicious forces of demons, who beckoned the people of the Balkans to dominate through supremacy.

Sharing a common cultural, religious, and linguistic bond with Africa, Atlantis was far from an ordinary city. This majestic island, a landmass larger than Crete itself, was surrounded by a calming ocean horizon that spanned the distance.

The seemingly mythical utopian society of Atlantis endured in the tales spread by the Cretans. Yet, it was impossible to overlook such a dominant force that built an impressive empire. The politics and military traditions of Atlantis were handed down to their descendants, the Minoans, who carried within them a desire to free those trapped in slavery.

The story of Atlantis, a land of breathtaking beauty during a golden age of prosperity, continued to captivate the minds of Greek and Roman philosophers. In their descriptions, Atlantis was depicted as an immense kingdom larger than Libya and Asia Minor combined, located at the Straits of Gibraltar. This strategic point connects the Atlantic Ocean to the Mediterranean Sea and separates Europe from Africa, at the farthest reaches of the Mediterranean.

Ya-Uli, an Atlantean high priest, described how the gods of the fifth heavens sank the lost continent of Atlantis:

> *"Now, in Atlantis, there was a great empire which ruled over the whole island and several others... This vast power, gathered into one, endeavoured to subdue...the whole region... She was pre-eminent in courage and military skill and the leader of the Hellenes. And when the rest fell off from her, being compelled to stand alone, after having undergone the very extremity of dangers, she defeated and triumphed over invaders, and preserved from slavery those who were not yet subjugated, and generously liberated all the rest of us who dwelt within the pillars. But afterwards, there occurred violent earthquakes and floods, and in a single day and night of misfortunate, all warlike men sank into the earth, and the island of Atlantis in like manner disappeared in the depths of the Sea."*

For generations, an enchanting prosperity thrived until divine beings pierced the Mediterranean coast. The once prosperous lands of Atlantis and Crete, along with their trading partners, faced both spiritual and physical challenges from the Greek Pantheon deities. Soon after, white settlers from the north quickly covered the Aegean region, leading to an epic clash involving both earthly and celestial powers that turned the Mediterranean into a cosmic battlefield. Heavenly corruption among angelic beings sparked a conflict between the evil forces of the fifth heaven and the sons of light from the seventh heavens, causing chaos in the celestial world.

The once peaceful island of Atlantis shattered as the earth's crust tore open, unleashing molten lava from its depths. Darkness engulfed the day, with ominous clouds and thundering waves reaching for the heavens. A dormant volcano roared to life, silencing countless Atlanteans and Minoans of Crete forever.

The oozing lava spread like searing honey, smothering villages and cascading into the ocean. A fiery chain reaction of volcanic eruptions emerged with billowing smoke, raging infernos, and red-hot boulders propelled by nature's ferocity. Tremors unleashed monstrous tidal waves that soared up to 700 feet high. All of a sudden, the wrathful earth devoured numerous boats and fishing vessels in a nightmarish vortex of terror.

Chaos erupted across the landscape! The clouds unleashed a fierce torrent of gusting winds, instilling widespread dread. Atlantis gradually separated from its moorings, disintegrating like sand particles in the wind. Within a single day, the once-magnificent Atlantis vanished into nothingness. The mysterious civilization near Crete's shores would fade from memory.

In this world governed by forces from the fifth heavens, someone had to pay the price. The enigmatic outer gods orchestrated a malicious game designed to sow suffering and division. Their objective: conquer Earth by subdividing humanity into two factions - a superior class loyal to the fifth heavens, and an inferior class subjected to unmitigated oppression. Enjoying deep bonds and financial rewards from the fifth heavens, the superior class flourished despite their hardship.

Lucifer, the blazing Prince of Darkness forged from smokeless fire, was believed to rule this fifth realm. As commander of the mutinous angels and celestial guardians, he held influence over the universe. Out of all the Angels of Vengeance in their hierarchy, his serpentine form was the first to defy the Creator.

Lucifer, the defiant head angel, refused to submit to a new creation crafted from dark clay. His arrogance led him to challenge the idea, "Why should a Son of Fire kneel before a Son of Clay? I won't bow to a mortal made from black molded earth." Once a devoted servant of God, pride turned Lucifer into a traitor. A celestial battle emerged, resulting in those evil angels who despised humanity to be cast out.

Despite their fall, these demons found sanctuary in the lower heavens. This granted them the chance to defy the Creator, indulge in sin, and dedicate themselves to the fifth heavens. These fallen beings held a grudge against humanity. They targeted God's earthly creations with fear and deception while promoting pagan gods as superior beings.

Lucifer's serpentine figure stood above all other fallen angels. Most fire-bodied creatures had up to six wings and several heads filled with divine wisdom that terrified human minds. However, Lucifer, the blazing serpent, reigned as the highest authority in the fifth heavens – with not just six but thirty-six wings in total. The chief rebel angel possessed numerous eyes, which allowed him to cunningly identify his prey.

An intense battle unfolded between these spiritual forces in the outer world. Some endured conflict while following the sinister of rebellion; others fought with inner radiance, striving to please their Creator.

Defying the Creator may have seemed like an exercise of free will, but it was intertwined with a yearning to overthrow nature through demonic forces. Some, on the other hand, sought to honor the Creator by displaying unwavering loyalty, demonstrating their devotion to serving the Highest and battling the rogue angels of darkness.

This epic conflict in the world beyond wasn't merely a spiritual showdown between benevolent and malevolent entities. It had far-reaching implications on shaping human existence.

Raphael dwelled in the celestial realm of the seventh heaven, but his unforeseen downfall was unanticipated. Once a magnificent angel, he was banished from his heavenly home, stripped of his wings, and forced to roam the earth. Without any resentment or bitterness, he was only fueled by a deep curiosity about the human world.

Seeking refuge in the fifth heaven, Raphael, whose name signifies "healer" or "protector," symbolized the purest essence of a guardian angel. Known as "The Shining One Who Heals," he was amongst the seven angels responsible for guarding the Tree of Life in Eden.

As Raphael attempted to re-enter heaven's gates, he found himself lost and trapped between the outer world and earth. Desperate to overcome the spirits that blocked his way, he sought help from two unlikely allies – fallen angels Lilith and Eris of the fifth heaven. Together, they relieved him from unbearable agony.

However, their actions came at a cost: Eris was demoted to an ordinary deity after being whisked away into fifth heaven for aiding Raphael; while Lilith became a wanted fugitive who lost her ability to transform into spiritual light.

Guided by her own set of rules and exacting vengeance, when necessary, Lilith helped Raphael escape a violent priest's wrath and ended up becoming his trusted companion on a lengthy ministerial journey. Eventually defying and estranging herself from fifth heaven's authority, she chose to live among mortal humans. In each other's eyes, both Raphael and Lilith were outsiders now.

Banished from the seventh heavens, Raphael and Lilith, a fugitive from the fifth heavens, found unity through a test of faith. When Lilith regained her invisibility powers, she evaded guards, living secretly in a dungeon's shadows.

Blessed with captivating beauty, Lilith could take physical form as long as she remained loyal to the external world of the fifth heavens. She and Raphael fell in love but were torn apart by a shipwreck near Africa's coast. Raphael, chained, was taken to Egypt's royal palace in Thebes.

The tsunamis' devastating impact led to the disappearance of Atlantis and wreaked havoc on Crete. This cataclysmic event unleashed spiritual forces that empowered the Balkans to assert global dominance—an age marked by violence and emerging rivalries centered on race, customs, and religion.

In ancient Egyptian history, this period fashioned the Eighteenth Dynasty. With influences from Crete's Minoans and the Israelites, the empire underwent revitalization during the New Kingdom era and introduced remarkable personalities.

Under this dynasty, Egypt overcame the Hyksos invasion and united Upper and Lower Egypt. This age of prosperity produced two remarkable female pharaohs: Hatshepsut "the female falcon" and Neferneferuaten, better known as Nefertiti.

This era witnessed extraordinary artistic innovations, polytheistic religion expansion, and military triumphs, which brought new customs and ideas into Egyptian lands.

Some of the most extraordinary characters appeared in the New Kingdom on the African coast and throughout the Nile Delta. There was the radical Akhenaten and his mysterious wife, Queen Nefertiti, who captivated the heart of the empire with charisma and beauty, to his son, one of the most famous pharaohs, King Tutankhamun, also known as King Tut.

There was also Prince Moses, born of Israelite blood but raised as an Egyptian, who followed a path to worship his one and only God at a time when polytheistic deities overran the nation. His complexion was dark, resembling the Egyptians, due to living in the dry heat of the Mediterranean.

The heretic Akhenaten, and his wife, Nefertiti, abandoned the polytheistic gods with revolutionary changes, worshipping a new monotheistic deity called Aten, the radiant disc of the sun.

The nation was distracted by the gods of the outer world, who forced a deep division throughout the Egyptian Empire and took away the Israelites' special citizen status.

The Eighteenth Dynasty brought a series of plagues, including a curse of death, which darkened Egypt's sky for its disobedience.

In many ways, this new world sprung from the eruptions destroying Atlantis and Crete and sending tidal waves across the Mediterranean, ushering in a new world order of paganism. This transformation introduced various religious sects to the Mediterranean region.

The Minoan Golden Age came to an end, triggering a massive migration into Egypt and the Nile Delta. As a result, the Egyptians lost their two major trading partners, and Eurocentrism emerged and flourished throughout the Mediterranean.

When settlers from the Balkans arrived, they introduced a capitalist system that seemed to benefit Indo-European migrants. At its core, Eurocentric capitalism revolved around trading in an open market to gain economic power. However, this commerce wasn't always peaceful - sometimes it involved deception, theft, or even war.

Sadly, Africans or those with any degree of blackness were excluded from participating in this free market. Their valuable natural resources were exploited by merchants, pirates, corrupt clerical officials, or power-hungry commanders whose primary goal was to maintain dominance.

The plan was simple: keep African resources out of the hands of black Africans and control the resources as much as possible. There was no justice!

It appears that the entire world embraced the new economic system of capitalism, which consequently relegated Africans to a lower social class. Pagan gods seemed to vehemently encourage anti-blackness in the worst way. The fifth heavens initiated a movement to prohibit individuals with any degree of blackness from partaking in the capitalist free market or attaining success in the Eurocentric commercial world.

As a result, countless Africans plunged further into self-loathing and attempted to alleviate their suffering by adopting European lifestyles through imagined involvement in the system that ensnared them. Numerous African leaders engaged in this by exchanging whiskey for war prisoners, sexual concubines, or a small amount of coinage that gave them an illusion of power in the free market.

Confined in makeshift prisons, enslaved captives awaited their fate as European buyers prepared to purchase them from the packed and congested cells. Bound by chains, these individuals then faced terrifying voyages aboard slave ships towards various corners of the earth. This brutal trade acted as a catalyst, turning the European free market economy into a global juggernaut.

The Balkan settlers embarked on a journey to colonize vast regions of the Mediterranean and parts of Africa in overseas ventures, driven by a negative perception of blackness. As they seized territories around the Mediterranean, they exploited its natural resources for their own gain. To maintain their dominance, they devised rules and deceitful practices that hindered Africans from participating in the free market, bolstering the invaders' devotion to the divisive gods of the fifth heavens.

These mysterious forces from the fifth heavens cast a dark shadow over justice and perpetuated an ever-shifting hierarchy of values. The ultimate objective was to amass wealth by perpetuating poverty and draining resources. This marked the beginning of an enduring revolution characterized by political chaos, bloodshed, and an ongoing struggle for liberation and freedom that would span generations.

CHAPTER 1

THERE IS A SPECIAL calling for angels in the physical and spiritual realms. The starkest comparison between the angels of light and the angels of darkness is the importance of supernatural blessings that benefit the most loyal followers. In most cases, the differences are expressed in our daily lives with love, kindness, and compassion toward each other.

However, in the calamity of history and the present day, the angels of darkness represent a silent hierarchy of human classification. This ranking allows the fifth heavens to rule the earthly domain like magic.

Accepting the dark side of our spiritual adolescence to embrace the rules of the fifth heavens is conspiring with wickedness. On the other hand, the divinatory growth that directs us toward a strict path of positive action becomes pleasant and fulfills our obligation to the seventh heavens.

The dark forces of angelic beings rule the fifth heavenly realm, while higher powers of angels and archangels of the light rule the seventh heavens.

The corruption of angelic beings after the creation of humanity became the central theme of divine knowledge and reverence, directing the mind toward the fifth heavens instead of the mysterious and omnipotent creator, Yahweh, whose throne is high above the seventh heavens. This Creator is the only entity to whom the fifth heavens would swiftly bow or kneel.

This mysterious, supreme Creator, for the most part, plays a silent role in the corruption of the natural order of the cosmic world. But a seamless web of life is associated with every victory against the fifth heavens and the demonic spirits of darkness.

At last, otherworldly forces infiltrated Earth, bringing corruption and materialistic temptations as a sign of their willingness to cooperate with the celestial beings from beyond. The foremost prince of the fallen angels, commanding legions of outcasts, had human counterparts who willingly chose to join the sinister aspects of humanity. This alliance allowed these fallen angels to flourish without consequences.

In a twisted manner, the essence of the fifth heavens infiltrated the invaders from the Balkans, driving them to commit vile acts of violence against innocent people. All this was done to appease their extraterrestrial deities without any fear of retribution. This territorial dispute resulted in an ongoing generational battle, awash with terror and bloodshed, as the fifth heavens sought dominion over all others.

A celestial conflict erupted between the forces of the fifth and seventh heavens: the agents of the fifth heavens squaring off against warriors of light. Caught between these two realms was Raphael, an angel hailing from the seventh heavens, torn between both worlds.

The Divine Power chose Raphael to lead humanity who had turned away from their glorious Creator. He was selected because of a desire to embrace the fifth heavens with love born before their fall from grace. The love for the fallen angels and the adoration for humanity never disappeared.

Guided by two fiery Archangels, Raphael descended from the highest heavens through the celestial spheres, eventually reaching Earth without wings. He sought sanctuary in a temple located in Pergamon, a city on the Mediterranean's western coast.

Soon, Pergamon emerged as a hub for administration and culture, boasting three imperial temples and the Temple of Asklepios, dedicated to the Greek god of medicine. This transformation made Pergamon an influential center for the Hellenistic world.

Raphael's tale showcases the profound bond between the physical world and spirituality. Becoming an earthly being—comprised of substance, flesh, and bone—Raphael embodied an angel walking amongst humans, albeit without wings.

Raphael's fall from heaven was a divine gift, sending him on a mission to dismantle a system of hierarchy deeply ingrained in the world. Tragically, this cycle of violence estranged humanity from the Creator and the seventh heavens. Raphael became a shining light in the darkness of an unforgiving realm, yet people chose to follow the Angels of Evil over the Angels of Light.

Each step Raphael took stood as a challenge to the established power and a path towards liberation. While many succumbed to darkness, he fiercely advocated for justice and equality in alignment with the seventh heavens. Raphael transformed from an invisible, fiery spirit into a mortal figure, experiencing pain but gifted with a mystical inner eye. This third eye embodied the conscious mind's ability to peer into the depths of reality and create a connection between humanity and divine wisdom.

In essence, Raphael's life was a series of nightmares as he navigated a world consumed by carnal desires and pleasure, something he had only observed from afar while in heaven. Adding to his struggles was Lucifer, the powerful Prince of Darkness who reigned over the fifth heavens. As leader of pagan deities, Lucifer blamed humanity for his own fall from grace. Even so, Angels were bound by their duty to serve the Creator without engaging in evil or defying orders while residing in the seventh heavens.

Lucifer was told to bow before the new creation made of black sculpted clay. His pride and lust for power wouldn't allow the rebel angels to prostrate before God's new creation formed out of black earth. Lucifer and his legions of angels were cast out of the seventh heavens like lightning.

A mild breeze of vengeance brought Raphael face to face with the dark side of humanity. His dreams filled his eyes with tears. The strain of anguish haunted him as though he was estranged from his angelic identity.

The memories that made him immortal were gone. His old life had gone away completely. He could taste the morning air and everything that made him human. Raphael could feel his human existence—as flesh, and the desire to live a mortal life became permanent in his mind.

The epic clash between the realms of the fifth and seventh heavens transcended a mere spiritual conflict among angelic beings. Earth transformed into an arena where control over humanity's fate hung in the balance, and Raphael found himself entangled in the ensuing pandemonium. Harmonious voices – both virtuous and nefarious – infiltrated his mind, enticing him to drift into dreams. His thoughts shone like brilliant flames.

Lilith, an ethereal entity from the fifth heavens, initially resisted Raphael's vision. Nevertheless, her inner light began to guide her. The Creator instilled free will within the angels, granting them the chance to tread darker paths. Embittered by their choices, some renegade angels strayed too far from redemption and refused to return to the Light. Raphael's fervent yearning for Lilith might be the very reason he lost his wings.

Despite residing in separate spiritual realms and possessing divine prowess, their rivalry often incited intense friction between them. However, over time, their spiritual energies intertwined, conspiring on a unified trajectory. Raphael harbored an ardent infatuation for Lilith, whose allure once captivated Adam with erotic love.

Lilith, a queen in her own right, overthrew nations and had the power to shift from a dazzling spiritual figure to the most enchanting woman.

Alongside Eris, the goddess of conflict, Lilith was among the spirits that Raphael encountered before the fallen angels' descent. Raphael endured numerous trials on Earth before regaining his angelic form.

Blessed with prophetic abilities, Raphael was haunted by terrifying dreams and visions of exiled angels and celestial beings from the seventh heavens. His thoughts were consumed with the seventh heaven until the sounds of the fifth heavens attempted to counterbalance its impact. Unbeknownst to Raphael and Lilith, their struggles radiated hope upon common people as they gained power and influence over nations' fate.

In reality, Raphael was one of the higher celestial beings from the seventh heavens sent to elevate humanity's consciousness. The Creator adored the human world so deeply that various angels and archangels were dispatched to alter their behavior.

The sinister forces of the fifth heavens attempted to dominate Raphael's life through bloodshed and unspeakable acts of violence. In his conscious mind, faint whispers lingered behind each thought he had. Raphael found himself caught in an internal struggle for truth, unsure which side of the conflict was reaching out to him.

Visions from the fifth heavens tempted Raphael with worldly pleasures, while revelations from the highest realms granted him wisdom, might, and bravery to resist falling prey to humanity's corrupt inclinations. Nevertheless, he grappled with his emotions and the daunting task of navigating a mortal existence. His very survival was endangered by the horrific savagery plaguing the Mediterranean. This brutal persecution and torment were sanctioned under the new laws imposed by the invaders.

Desperate to make sense of this horrendous reality, Raphael turned to prayer, seeking solace in day and night conversations with a higher power. The fifth heavens possessed a voracious hunger for extreme malevolence that defied all ethical norms, standing in opposition to humanity's innate desire to revere and serve their Creator.

In a sense, all the world's desires and pleasures were intertwined in the process of transformation from the earthly realm to the spiritual world. It was a sad time, and his mission seemed too big. There was a religious rivalry in the angelic orders with the pagan gods in a constant battle to destroy humanity. The seventh heavens were responsible for saving humanity, and Raphael became a Savior to strengthen the human understanding of the Creator.

There was so much poverty, depression, and bloodshed on earth. He didn't know normalcy or have the ability to live his new life as a mortal. His strange life of aches and pain came as swiftly as his fall from the seventh heavens. Raphael felt a deep sense of brotherhood on earth and had to convince mortals to save themselves from self-destruction.

Raphael found himself in a bizarre situation. His entrance into the physical world was just as jarring as losing his wings, leaving him powerless. The pain and sorrow of his predicament stood in stark contrast to the celestial glow of his heavenly abode. Yet, the angelic forces of the fifth heaven seemed intent on tearing humanity apart like a catastrophic epidemic.

A considerable distinction existed between the deeds of malicious and light angels. Nevertheless, the enchanting allure of the fifth heaven allowed earthly desires and seductive powers to bend the concept of free will. No compassion could be found among them. The invaders from the Balkans appeared ensnared in a sinister trap, directed by an unseen force.

Whispers from the highest realm of angels reached Raphael, reminding him of his mission and advising him to resist the allure of lower beings. Yet, his longing for Lilith only intensified, progressively isolating him from the divine connection he once felt with the exalted angels. Eventually, their hushed voices receded from his consciousness, failing to retain his attention.

The looming prospect of chaos and unease was undeniable. But simultaneously, Raphael's life began to evolve in ways he had never anticipated. On one side was the danger of his soul drifting from its true nature; on the other were chilling glimpses into the dark side of human existence – racism and inequality.

Raphael found himself tossed about in a storm of emotions, torn between love for higher beings, relentless dreams, and turmoil in the material world. Death was all around him, and his very soul seemed to be engulfed in flames of anguish. In the midst of this tribulation, Raphael could not silence the indelible yearning for tranquility.

Suddenly, a tender voice questioned him: "What do you know about mortal man?" All at once, everything fell silent as Raphael raised his eyes toward the voice's source. Unsure whether he was imagining it or not, he hesitated momentarily.

For an instant, Raphael's face twisted into an expression of fright; it seemed as if terror had paralyzed him. His eyes widened as he concentrated on listening to this voice that had seemingly emerged out of nowhere. Catching his breath after such a shock, he wondered if these were just more fallen angels from the lower realm attempting to inflict further pain upon him.

He looked up, tilting his head as he heard the peculiar voices and saw a towering human-like silhouette with dark, heavy wings.

Soon after, the sky came into view, and Raphael became entranced as he observed the forsaken souls of the mortal world, traded like livestock to enhance the lives of the affluent. These images of despair distracted him from the uncanny experiences that awaited the indigenous people of the Aegean. Yet, it was everything imaginable for those who defied taking part in Lucifer and his fallen angels' corrupt endeavors.

The scene was cataclysmic. Winds and rain exceeded 200 miles per hour, battering a community situated beyond the Strait of Gibraltar, where the Atlantic Ocean meets the Mediterranean Sea. Blood spilled from the victims, and the waters consumed the idyllic island of Atlantis. The enigmatic event eradicated Atlantis within the expansive blue ocean—a never-before-witnessed horror.

The atmosphere in the Baltic region turned warmer and muggier—a stark contrast to the climate that fostered centuries of peace and collaboration between African and European peoples.

As the glaciers retreated across Europe's grasslands, adventurous settlers journeyed towards the Baltic shores and ventured south to the Aegean. Unaware of the colossal icebergs floating nearby, they were caught off guard when temperatures plummeted. The icebergs' approach to Atlantis brought increasingly harsh weather to a land that had been warm and humid. The climate changed significantly due to these icy behemoths.

Dark clouds filled the sky, while a divine northern wind accompanied a warm breeze from distant realms. Sunlight reached the north, causing massive ice sheets to melt and unleash enormous glaciers into the frigid waters of the North Atlantic Ocean. As the sea level surged, sandy beaches were submerged, and raging waves decimated coastal towns and villages. The once bustling harbors and settlements transformed drastically as giant ice caps continued to melt.

With no barrier between Africa and Europe, there was nothing to stop the migration from the Balkans. The stage was set for new settlers to savagely oppress their neighbors with help from the gods of the outer world.

Atlantis's residents battled the encroaching waters, clueless about the bizarre events that lay ahead. Powerful waves, akin to mountains, crashed onto the shore. Icebergs barreled towards the coast at breakneck speeds, reminiscent of towering peaks. As ice melted, refreshing winds swept through and sea levels ascended. Earthquakes and floods devoured Atlantis and its brave dwellers, as colossal tidal waves over six hundred feet high pummeled the island at the behest of deities from the fifth heavens.

The winds shifted, directing their force at the grand city of Atlantis. Cosmic energy battered the ill-fated island in an apocalyptic storm-like manner, annihilating its beauty with relentless rage. Volcanoes erupted with blistering lava while a hailstorm of viscous mud and sulfur poured down from above. In conclusion, a devastating earthquake unleashed a tsunami that consumed all life in its path, leaving nothing but devastation and silence.

A terrifying blend of scorching lava, volcanic ash, and heated rocks burst from deep within the Earth's mantle. The once-Prince of Air, Lucifer, unleashed his wrath upon Atlantis' islands, calling upon his sinister cohorts to decimate the Aegean citizens. The scorching lava flowed relentlessly, striking nearby coastal cities and leaving devastation in its wake. This horrific event was forever deemed "The Night of Horror."

As volcanic plumes tarnished the once-gorgeous capital city, the sea and sky united under a covering of hot lava. Dark clouds gathered above the coastline, transforming the rain into gleaming, swords of death.

The chaos created a suffocating darkness as thick black ash filled the air and settled all around. It seemed as though fury itself had descended from the heavens.

The gods of the fifth heavens sought to conquer the earth with all the barbarity and cruelty imaginable.

Legend states that a mighty power came out of the Atlantic Ocean to inflict punishment on the entire island of Atlantis. The Atlanteans had some of the most brilliant fighting militias in the Mediterranean before they suddenly perished.

A series of underground earthquakes, each carrying a dreadful storm, had mysteriously destroyed the beautiful island in the Atlantic. The weather didn't improve until Atlantis vanished. The eruption lasted for hours, followed by torment of rain and rivers dense with mud that swallowed entire villages.

In the glaring light of day, an oppressive darkness descended upon Atlantis, as if nighttime had arrived unbidden. Thunder roared with fury, consuming boats and fishing vessels in a terrifying whirlwind. Enormous waves invaded the land, swallowing the areas near the ports in under a minute as the sea surged above ground level.

The catastrophic volcanic eruption and ensuing tsunamis stripped away any semblance of power from the once-elite Atlanteans. No longer could they claim mastery over navigation and trade, nor boast of Atlantis being the Mediterranean's crown jewel or the pinnacle of technological advancement.

With devastating speed, clouds of destruction enveloped the mountainous Aegean Islands, leaving a desolation akin to nuclear ruin. This relentless calamity silenced many Atlantean citizens.

As doom loomed over Atlantis, its inhabitants remained trapped like birds awaiting their fate at the hands of merciless captors. Their fleeting hope lay with divine intervention from the seventh heavens.

CHAPTER 2

THE BALKAN INVADERS SOUGHT to rebuild Crete into their social order by eliminating the original Aegean culture. The wrath of the fifth heavens descended upon Crete's seven cities, marking the beginning of a ruthless demolition. Amidst the scorching heat and stifling humidity, a violent bloodbath ensued as the enigmatic power of the fifth heavens altered everything.

As dawn approached, Balkan soldiers hastened to penetrate the city walls, igniting a fierce battle. These intruders brimmed with creative vigor, rapidly shifting the balance of power. The carnage also paved the way for new economic prospects for the Balkan settlers. Meanwhile, no mercy was shown to the indigenous inhabitants; even innocent children weren't spared from the brutality.

The invading forces advanced through towns, ruthlessly attacking women and children who resisted their incursion. Several captives met grisly fates, either having their throats slashed by swords or being offered as human sacrifices to priests. Invaders went from one house to another, setting buildings ablaze and conducting savage street raids while prisoners pleaded for mercy. The vengeance of the fifth heavens were unleashed on the seven cities of Crete.

The brutal conquest of Crete commenced, followed by a horrific bloodbath as the intense battle unfolded in the sweltering, humid weather. The ominous power of the fifth heavens altered everything!

The cycle of violence erupted before daybreak when Balkan soldiers charged to breach the city walls. These invaders from the Balkans arrived with relentless force, causing a dramatic shift in power from the very beginning. Consequently, new economic prospects emerged for the Balkan settlers. However, no sympathy was shown towards the native residents, and even innocent children were not spared from these atrocities.

As the invading settlers stormed through each town, they viciously attacked women and children resisting them. Some captives faced a gruesome fate—slaughtered by swords or used as human sacrifices for their priests. The ruthless settlers went from one house to another, setting ablaze buildings while dragging their victims into numerous blood-stained street ambushes. Desperate pleas for mercy filled the air but fell on deaf ears.

No compassion was shown to women, children, or elders in this devastating conflict. Women were violated before their own children's tearful eyes as their husbands were mercilessly slain by the soldiers. The remaining populace, who were unfortunate enough to avoid the nightmare, were sold into slavery, providing unpaid labor across the Empire.

Their cherished cities burned relentlessly until they eventually crumbled to ashes. Citizens faced excruciating deaths through sacrificial burnings, being trampled by horsemen, or hanging on poles scattered throughout the towns. The Aegean people were utterly unaware of the reasons behind the attacks on their villages.

New settlers cornered the food supply, causing the people of Lydia to perish from starvation. Some fleeing soldiers managed to find refuge in Ethiopia and other North African nations. The daily violence endured by helpless victims became a grim routine for these Balkan newcomers, as though they had received divine permission without any celestial objections.

Oppression became a common sight against the native inhabitants of Crete, but it couldn't compare to the horrifying massacre that ensued. Streets were overwhelmed with corpses as a result of spiraling unrest. The appalling genocide took on a recreational tone while young children screamed relentlessly. Shouts and uproar filled the air from the beginning, and the brutal carnage engulfing the Aegean Islands seemed essential to appease higher powers.

Marked by a deadly curse, the gods of the fifth heavens celebrated each triumph. Natives continued to flee the carnage brought upon Crete by the Indo-Aryan invasion. The clamor of war drums filled the air and bloodthirsty settlers' spears fell like rain. Swarming over the land like dark clouds, these invaders brought death wherever they went. Countless lives were crushed under the weight of an evil spirit's campaign of terror.

The moment the invaders reached the cities of Crete, they slaughtered their way into residential houses, burned victims alive, and sacrificed children to the gods of the fifth heavens. There were so many tears.

The Cretans experienced a harsh reality, as they were treated like prey by the merciless gods of the fifth heavens. As a result, the Aegean region transformed into a crimson graveyard in the name of divinity. Rampaging through the land, the invaders from the Balkans obliterated entire ecosystems, demolished libraries, and ultimately enslaved the indigenous peoples.

These conquerors believed that destiny had granted them divine status and entitlement to all the riches and luxuries within their reach, free from consequences. Often regarded as enigmatic beings with seemingly supernatural abilities, they wielded powerful spears and horse-driven chariots capable of eliminating any creature or human from a distance.

With these extraordinary armaments at their command, they exercised control over life and death and maintained authority with only a small force. They traversed mountainous terrains and valleys, leaving no chance for the inhabitants to escape or avoid their brutal onslaught. This conflict solidified the integration of the fifth heavens with the physical realm while also ensuring that symbolic statues celebrating spiritual power dominated in more distant territories.

Although materialistic in nature, their diverse battle strategies enabled these Balkan settlers to establish dominance over Crete's coastal islands. The conquest of Crete's seven cities posed a considerable challenge as they sought global supremacy.

After a catastrophic volcanic eruption, Smyrna was the first city to experience a brutal attack owing to its central and strategically vital position on the Aegean coast which connected it with mainland territories. Diverse tribal groups from the Balkan Mountain region joined forces to assume control over Crete. Known as "The First City of Asia," this historical urban center became home to a loosely affiliated Balkan confederation that conquered various Mediterranean and Aegean islands.

A significant flaw of the original inhabitants was their openness to let outsiders blend into their culture and faith. The once great cities of Crete fell rapidly under foreign control. As they resisted the invading Balkan settlers, the conflict only grew more intense.

In a blink of an eye, the nation was sacrificed, and countless lives were lost. Chaos ensued as Cretan leaders faced imprisonment or death. Fear gripped the people as the Balkan settlers displayed a barbaric nature, devoid of honor and leadership, fostering hatred and resentment towards Crete's native population.

Rapid heartbeats pulsed wildly under the bright moonlight. Cities drowned in tears as the battle for territory turned into a deadly trap. Towering waves surged past Gibraltar and the Pillars of Hercules, reaching the mysterious unknown. Observing intently, Raphael watched Balkan settlers arrive to support the enigmatic deities of the fifth heavens.

On makeshift boats, the invaders swiftly conquered Crete and nearby islands, adeptly transporting horses and chariots. They stormed the shores with unparalleled speed, wielding double-edged swords. The inhabitants of Crete's seven cities succumbed to their power, weakened by recent natural disasters.

Chaos from the destruction opened the door for this invasion. Desperate, Raphael sought help from the angels of the seventh heavens to curb the evil brewing in by the fifth heaven, only to be met with silence. As a last resort, he prayed at the temple, seeking strength to aid Crete's vulnerable people.

Out of nowhere, Lilith emerged, stunning and captivating as she interrupted Raphael's plea. "Raphael, our cherished temple has been tainted by demonic forces. This is none other than the Temple of Zeus, the leader of the Olympian gods," she vividly detailed.

With great surprise, Lilith guided Raphael towards the priest. He carefully ascended the magnificent staircase, adorned with sapphire stones. Upon reaching the top, he discovered a sacred chamber reserved only for priests.

A noise came from behind a door, followed by a male voice questioning their intentions. Lilith retreated as Raphael approached the source of the voice. She remained silent and distanced herself further while the man's high-pitched voice continued.

Raphael explained, "I am an angel from the seventh heaven who once wielded immense power. I was sent to Earth to make peace between humans and other angelic beings. My heart is heavy, and my prayers unanswered. I seek respite within this temple for a short time."

Scoffing, the voice replied, "This is hallowed ground, accessible only to fifth heaven angelic hierarchies. I recognize you, Raphael—a fallen angel from the seventh heaven. You've become mortal in body and spirit, bereft of your wings. A common man seeking refuge has no place here."

Raphael turned around to run but was captured by two temple guards. Lilith leaped into the air in a fury, fleeing the scene through an opened window. Raphael was thrown into a dungeon and tortured for being a traitor.

As it happened, he entered the jail dungeon for swift retribution. Again, his prayers were denied as he fell into darkness. The punishment crushed his spirit like a moth.

There in the prison cell, the nightmares would never cease. He tried to wiggle free, but the dreams kept haunting him night after night.

He kept twisting and turning but could never run away. He heard himself scream to exhaustion as the dreams became too real. Raphael finally realized that he must look to the heavens for inner strength as no one understood him except for the seventh heavens.

Raphael's life was flipped entirely. He had been enticed into a world brimming with wealth, yet the dark side of this realm brought a sour feeling to his heart. His inner thoughts blazed like sudden bursts of fire.

There was a moment's pause as Raphael remembered the peace and the feeling of love and safety in the seventh heavens. He remembered his time in the heavens, and his anger surged into happiness. He wasn't alone, and deep down, he could feel the eternal presence of the magnificent seventh heavens.

In a deep sleep, he could still see the seventh heavens. He loved those dreams of peace that comforted him. It was beautiful and full of love. But the dreams didn't last long. The vision always suddenly vanished.

A sudden lightning flash jolted Raphael awakes, his vision dissipating. He sprang up, only to slump down on the bed, overwhelmed with distress. Inhaling deeply, he tried to gather his scattered thoughts. Emotions raced through him; a strong sense of faith rooted deeply within. Dazed and in pain, his knees quivered.

Surveying the cramped prison cell brought him back to reality, intensifying his loneliness and discomfort. How long had he been asleep? The dream provided a fleeting respite from the horrors of incarceration, allowing him a glimpse of the joy and serenity found in the ethereal seventh heavens.

Tormented by the fleeting nature of life, tears flowed down his face as he wrestled with feelings of insignificance and frustration. Struggling for breath, the fear of being denied entry to heaven haunted him persistently. Even during his waking hours, echoes of angelic voices and celestial hymns resonated in his ears.

Baffled by celestial disruptions, Raphael couldn't fathom why people sought the outer world of the fifth heaven for their protection. Overwhelmed with shame for his frailty, he battled to break free from mortal constraints but to no avail. Day and night he prayed, yet his pleas went unanswered, leaving him feeling utterly trapped.

Bewildered by the newcomer's control over life and death, his mind was tormented by prophetic visions of future events. The unsettling imagery heightened his fear, amplifying the ongoing power struggle for dominance in the region.

Tormented by a vivid imagination, he experienced an array of nuanced emotions. However, with time, his voice gradually faded until it was completely silenced. The world around him appeared to be engulfed in turmoil.

Imprisoned in darkness both physically and mentally, Raphael felt as though the spiritual realm of the fifth heavens had devoured the world, leaving no hope for escape. The threat of madness loomed over his thoughts. Struggling to shift his mindset from vengeance to forgiveness, Raphael found his wisdom clouded by emotions.

With eyes clenched tight, he felt a surge of unrelenting anger. His dark brown eyes glinted as his body trembled from the overwhelming thoughts consuming him. Shame and guilt mingled in the night air, causing his eyes to sparkle. Although his soul's pain persisted, fear continued to haunt his thoughts. He had never imagined that rage and frustration could wield such control over him.

He realized that the world was shrouded in darkness, the moral universe suffering an immense blow from above. Was there anything more than endless pain and death? It was a bitter struggle to find any light amid the shadows. As he learned of the horrifying genocide against the native people, his anguish only grew, pacing incessantly in his jail cell.

Tormented by nightmares, visions, and prophecies searing into his very soul, he experienced no ordinary dreams. These heavy thoughts weighed on him while those in power dismissed his insights. The dreams foretold the fate of a world under siege by settlers claiming new territories. The Aegean region was now controlled by white settlers from the Balkans.

Raphael could not change this outcome and found himself teetering on the brink of death. The nightmares were relentless, and evil persisted against the Cretans. Fearful of the overpowering dreams, he sometimes dreaded falling asleep.

Raphael had no answer for the bloodshed or large-scale oppression by the new Eurocentric authority. The harmony was broken, and the invaders had no sympathy.

At times, divine creatures appeared like bright flames of fire. They spoke with a bold authority but of nothing that might indicate what side of the battle they represented. Nothing in their character suggested some wrath.

Swarming from the Balkans, invaders targeted Ephesus, a gem among Mediterranean cities brimming with wealth. The local populace found themselves demoted to second-class citizens, as these foreign conquerors divvied up their abundant farmlands. United in purpose, the Avenging Angels of the fifth heavens and the Balkan settlers appeared to share a single soul.

The natives of Crete saw their beautiful city come to a tragic end by being set ablaze by the newcomers. They had no control over the outcome. Their freedom had been snatched away so suddenly and unexpectedly.

So many bodies lay dead. Lives were brutally turned upside down. No matter what, the dark and gloomy dominance of the fifth heavens turned the Aegean into a sea of fire.

Raphael pondered the possibility of reaching out to the Ethiopians to save Crete from captivity, but he found himself imprisoned in a dark, unfamiliar dungeon, feeling just as confined as the Cretans. As he gazed out of his cell, stormy war clouds loomed, threatening to engulf the Aegean in darkness. Chaos seemed to fill the entire world.

Within the dungeon, many inmates experienced the perks of being near an angel on earth. Raphael conversed with remarkable wisdom and performed wondrous healings while confined in his cell. As he grappled with his thoughts day and night in what appeared to be an epic battle between good and evil forces, he saw no hope of escape.

Raphael quickly gained the admiration of his fellow prisoners and used his prophetic talents to earn the esteem of officials. His visions were straightforward, and at times, his revelations seemed to align with the course of the pagan invaders.

At times, his visions seemed to do more harm than good. It was as though the Cretan's souls had been snatched away. There was no renewed spirit to move forward.

So many people in the Mediterranean world were like the living dead. They became hopeless in every way possible. Their liberty was snatched away, and the injustice became a terrifying nightmare. This was a new era of twisted evils and a cruel cycle of death and destruction.

Raphael's surreal visions revealed the emergence of Eurocentric power, and the imagery was laden with cautionary tales, sadness, and the proclamation of catastrophe. An air of doubt enveloped the country like a looming shadow.

His thoughts went around like a roulette wheel as if his sanity became dimmed by the arc of the rage. The evil gods had his mind pulsating with every heartbeat. However, his prophecies revealed the rebirth of the Aegean, the future of Africa, and how the entire Mediterranean world would blossom due to the acknowledgment of the sole creator, God.

Raphael took his extraordinary visions heartily. It was as though an entire world was lost in darkness. The invaders unleashed atrocity on every man, woman, and child living in Crete.

In a sense, Raphael was a messenger sent to warn the people of their transgression and how the violence against the Cretans would return to the newcomers tenfold.

Raphael crafted a plan to merge the conquered lands of Ethiopia with the prosperous Congo, providing both economic and military stability. He hesitated briefly, his intentions uncertain, yet within the grace period granted by the Creator. As an angel of the seventh heaven, he was prohibited from causing harm to even those who committed evil.

Soon, news of a temple devoted to Athena, the patron goddess, sent waves of terror throughout the region, with more temples arising in its wake. These new sanctuaries symbolized the deities of the fifth heavens, as mortal heroes gained a devoted following around their final resting places. Greek and Roman factions in the Aegean found themselves vying for dominance as the central hub of the Imperial Cult for these fifth heaven gods.

CHAPTER 3

IN A STRANGE TWIST of faith, Raphael was rescued by Lilith and Eris when they diverted the flow of the river to the entrance of the high walls that led into the Tullianum prison. This killed two of the guards.

Raphael emerged from a stupor and escaped bondage, while Eris was taken up to the fifth heavens in a whirlwind and stripped of her title, goddess of strife and warfare. Eris was reduced to the rank of a common deity for her participation in the escape.

On the run from the outer world, Lilith found herself stripped of her shape-shifting abilities by the authority of the fifth heavens. It was Raphael who convinced her to embrace the path of righteousness. With chaos escalating, fighting for a noble cause became increasingly vital.

Despite Lilith holding onto the age-old "eye for an eye" belief, humanity faced a choice: either to align themselves with the fifth or seventh heavens in this cosmic war. One thing was certain, though – victory would ultimately belong to God, who commands unwavering devotion.

A bit of Raphael's sanity came back after he escaped from the cruel injustices of the fifth heavens. It seemed like all his energy was absorbed in the dungeon of the prison cell, as if his liveliness had been siphoned away.

It was a terrible scene. Raphael was a human in the mortal world and full of anger he could never have imagined. When the anger diminished momentarily, he could maintain some peace deep within his soul. He confessed his rage, and then the nightmares ceased to exist.

An intense desire to venture into the mortal realm gripped Raphael, who was devoted to saving the world from evil. However, the settlers' allegiance to the fifth heavens inflicted suffering upon defenseless victims. During the peak of the conflict, blood cascaded like uncontested rainfall, stirring a bitter resentment that swept through like a tidal wave. Raphael found himself enveloped in despair.

The Balkan settlers laid the groundwork for genocide and imposed servitude, slavery, and tyranny on the inhabitants of Crete and Asia Minor. A string of triumphs imparted an air of worldliness to the settlers, as each battle seemed like a divine signal from otherworldly gods. The invaders delighted in making Cretans labor on their land and surrender their riches to satisfy their conquerors' appetites.

The oppressors, characterized by their coarse and rugged looks, pursued a furious crusade provoked by the fifth heavens. Their pale skin was deemed a mark of superiority, forging unity among the Balkan settlers in the quest for Cretan territory.

Though the Balkan invaders seemed to wield little power, they managed to unleash a mystical force by remaining faithful to the fifth heaven. This force was sustained as long as the natives were kept apart from their Creator. Allegiance to these gods granted protection, a taste of material wealth, and absolute control – as long as the seventh heaven remained uninvolved.

This intense struggle to seize land and riches in the Aegean Islands sparked fierce battles among different European tribes. Consequently, a ruthless extermination policy was set in motion by the fifth heaven but executed by the settlers themselves.

Following fierce battles among mainland tribes, the Mycenaean Greeks gradually conquered Crete and the nearby Aegean Islands.

They maintained their slave system over the Cretans, while some Minoans sought refuge along Africa's coastlines.

This set the stage for a widespread exploitative economic scheme that other Europeans would later adopt. Amidst the ever-changing Aegean world, the Mediterranean found itself divided by a thirst for vengeance.

This unfolding dynamic propelled these rulers to global prominence, intertwining them with pagan gods who formed a blind pact with invading settlers. By the end of this tumultuous period, the Greeks had successfully seized control of all the Aegean Islands and vast areas of Africa.

The impact of various tribal groups of Anglo-Saxons formed a systemic structure of slavery, human rights abuses, and a life of servitude to these new settlers out of the Balkans. However, the victories of bloodshed in its most extreme form gave way to allegiance to imperial cults.

The searing horror brought all manners of wealth for the aggressors as long as they bowed down to the fifth heavens. There were two opposing sides, and the mighty power of the seventh heavens could do nothing unless the natives bowed down to the creator God and served Him with all of their heart and soul. There was only one God for the Indigenous natives to worship, and their protection gradually drifted away from the Light when they mindlessly accepted the gods of foreigners.

The steady flow of invaders played a crucial role in misery, starvation, and disrespect for human lives. The invaders didn't change a thing! The intruding settlers continued the brutal and vicious treatment generation after generation and seized all the power away from the natives living in Crete.

This diabolical act of terror rained down on the inhabitants daily. The land was considered an entirely new world, representing the typical hierarchy of the gods given to the invaders by divine intervention. The pagan gods of the outer world gained fame after every victory of the Balkan settlers.

There was a dedication after each triumph to different gods or goddesses to glorify their cult lifestyle through the temple-building process. Religion and politics were integrated into a tyrannical government.

The wind changed course, granting the invaders an advantage and stripping away territory, concepts, and economic prosperity from the native inhabitants of Crete. It appeared as if a blazing river flowed through Crete's streets. The intruders embarked on a wild rampage of destruction.

The malevolent entities of the fifth heavens gleamed brightly above the Aegean, carrying out their mission of brutality. Every nation fell victim to the merciless fifth heavens, while the invasive colonizers from the Balkans ravaged the Aegean like ravenous beasts.

Over time, a universal system emerged, dividing humanity through sinful trade and prejudice. This motivated white settlers to strive for superiority by oppressing the native people. Gaining a higher status came with economic and financial benefits, obtained by enslaving enough victims under the guise of legality.

The ability to gain riches and honor was too tempting to ignore. The settlers took everything they pleased and gave glory to the fifth heavens. The violence was the worst thing the natives could've ever imagined.

There was a particular atmosphere that brewed over the horizon of the Mediterranean. While the Greeks were fighting over similar territories, other tribes from the Mountains of the Caucasus, such as the Assyrians, Babylonians, Persians, and the Hyksos, wandered throughout the Mediterranean. The Hyksos challenged the Egyptians for Lower Egypt and fought the natives living in Canaan.

Life along the Nile for Africans was disrupted by invasions from various Balkan tribes. These newcomers swept through the Mediterranean with an incredible force resembling the power of the fifth heavens. As they spread, they introduced a governance system focused on dividing people and imposing their own politics, economics, and culture.

These uninvited newcomers heralded the start of white-dominated power structures in the Mediterranean. Three mighty nations emerged from these clashes, each vying for global supremacy. The Balkan intruders embarked on a merciless crusade to rally support around the great sea and amass power. Their relentless brutality gave rise to the Babylonians, Persians, and Greeks, while the Hyksos merged with other Eurocentric tribes.

The Balkan settlers adopted much of the Cretan culture, enhancing its already stunning architecture and making the Greek civilization truly distinctive. With this new ruling system in place, native people were marginalized, and a ruthless division of humanity became accepted as the new norm for progress.

The settlers clung to their belief of superiority and found themselves, masters of their new-found territory, worshipping their silent partners from the fifth heavens. The white colonists became captives in illusion. The dominant culture in this new pyramid of power was simply a pawn for the fifth heavens to temporarily rule the earthly domain in the most horrible way possible.

When Crete finally fell, the Minoan civilization of old Europe, which practiced an agricultural and maritime way of life, was replaced with tribal settlers proficient in a nomadic way of life.

The savagery changed the lives of the natives. Arrows and spears rained down daily on the natives. Some natives became submissive to the new settlers and followed their pagan customs of worshipping the fifth heavens.

The rigid laws of the fifth heavens showed no favor to dark skin people, denying them equality and economic stability. The relentless cosmic evils sought injustice, making financial prosperity available only to those who submitted to the pagan deities of the outer world.

These fresh arrivals from the Balkan region once thrived as hunters and skilled nomads, stalking prey while carrying portable tents. Their experience in this enigmatic and ever-moving lifestyle transformed these long-haired, light-skinned conquerors into formidable warriors.

The Greeks adopted and excelled at the agricultural practices of the Minoans, expanding their influence to include the hilly areas where the Alban settled along the Tiber River.

They merged with their kindred Sabines, Latium, Romilia, and other tribes from the Balkans, as they gradually unified the communities on its famous seven hills. Incredible acts of horror poured out unbelievable wealth. This aggressive behavior turned the empire into a dominant power in the Mediterranean.

These wicked, wild men reaped incredible benefits from the evil they'd sown. Every day, enslaved people would toil the land to produce food, and gathered abundance of fruits, vegetables, raw materials, and minerals to satisfy the invader's lifestyle.

This made the Greeks very wealthy, so they became a powerful society within the new empire due to a high demand for food. The Greeks inherited the technological know-how and ingenuity of the Cretans and multiplied because of farming and the wealth of the neighboring communities.

In ancient Greek society, large farms were operated by enslaved individuals, leading to massive profits for the farm owners. The native Minoans, treated like mere pawns, possessed remarkable skills and inhabited one of the most fertile islands in the Mediterranean. As new invaders arrived, they began embracing novel ideas to boost the economy.

The Cretans were experts in numerous fields such as carpentry, pottery, jewelry-making, painting, weaving, metalworking, and even perfume production. They understood the importance of both irrigation and cultivation in maintaining their unique lifestyle. Balkan tribes harnessed the art of livestock cultivation to bring about a prosperous societal transformation.

These newly acquired abilities greatly enhanced metalworking techniques. Ancient Greeks took full advantage of the natives' skills by utilizing them for extensive ironwork projects that helped develop better warfare tools and agricultural progress. This period marked the birth of innovative tree felling methods, advanced construction techniques, and a harmonious melding of cultures within the Mediterranean region.

During the dawn of industrialism, the New Greek Empire experienced a major transformation with the rise of metals and ironworking. The Aegean region's cultural melting pot led to numerous innovations, yet it couldn't escape the clutches of poverty and anxiety.

Pagan temples speckled the outskirts of cities, drawing massive crowds who gathered to honor their chosen gods. These deities were celebrated through various ceremonies and festivals, connecting people with the divine forces beyond their world.

Mighty war gods Ares and Zeus held influential positions amongst the settlers, who believed invoking their wrath could unleash catastrophes on their enemies. Engaging in rituals to access the supernatural realm was a widespread practice, commonly pursued for guidance or power. In lush groves of Aricia, Artemis, the goddess of hunting, enjoyed devout worship and admiration from her followers.

The ancient Greeks recognized Mars as Ares and transformed Indra into Zeus. Diana was venerated in Aricia's woodland, and a shrine was constructed for her on the Aventine Hill, one of Rome's legendary Seven Hills. From the Caucasus mountains, the new Greek gods rapidly entered Cretan lands.

As if by magic, the pagan gods emerged from obscurity with shared connections. The heavenly deities formed an unbreakable alliance with the white settlers, casting a sinister shadow over the Mediterranean as they pursued a shared destiny. In no time, these Balkan settlers were imbued with boundless energy.

The rules of the fifth heaven were straightforward: no personal ties or empathy for the native inhabitants. These locals had no option but to pay homage to the otherworldly pagan gods. This enigmatic force aimed to draw people away from their Creator and guide them blindly toward the fifth heavens with blind understanding. Paganism spread across the Aegean and the Mediterranean like wildfire.

Something strange was happening in the Mediterranean. It was a spiritual phenomenon brought down by the gods of the fifth heaven. The evil eye of the fifth heavens continued silently while the colonizers pushed forward on the edge of madness.

Without exception, the great, invisible force of the fifth heavens illuminated the Aegean with chaos as though it were trying to catch up with time.

A gigantic vacuum arose throughout the Mediterranean, giving authority to bloodthirsty savages who brought new forms of misery to the dark-skinned people of the Mediterranean and the Nile Delta.

The colonizers allowed certain towns and villages political liberty while requiring them to pay a portion of their earnings to the Greek authorities.

This new polytheistic religious system brought about a significant change in the lives of the natives. A Eurocentric way of life became the standard of progress for people living in Crete or the New Greek territory.

Asserting their moral superiority, the inhabitants of the fifth heavens seized land and culture from those with darker features. This led to a widespread acceptance of imperialistic exploitation, as if it were divine gifts from the gods of the fifth heavens. The enigmatic religion of Dionysus was shrouded in clandestine rituals. As the latest addition to the twelve Olympians, Dionysus dwelled on Mount Olympus, safeguarding the emerging cities of the New World.

The Greek society believed that these revered deities resided in the distant fifth heavens alongside innumerable warriors. Those who transgressed the laws of the fifth heaven faced dire consequences—swift death or being thrown into a pit teeming with ferocious beasts. Amidst all this, Greek souls languished in darkness.

CHAPTER 4

RAPHAEL FEARLESSLY TRAVELED FROM one community to another, spreading the message of the seventh heavens and the Holy Creator with a fiery voice.

He argued that the fifth heavens' power was only temporary. It was inferior to the seventh heavens, and the Holy Creator had authoritative control over all creation.

One of the tasks was to persuade Lilith to stay on the side of the seventh heavens and the sole Creator of Life.

For the most part, Crete adopted the Greek culture, and soon a Eurocentric way of life dominated the Aegean Islands.

The people of the Mediterranean had a range of skin tones, from coal black to various shades of tan. Still, the Greeks believed they were the divine race to rule all humanity. This apparent dilemma brought a new cult into the region to appease the gods of the outer world.

Raphael was profoundly affected as the Cretans began to lose their cultural identity. There was no freedom or liberty for the natives. The newcomers were there to stay, and there was no escaping the carnage. The white masters were at the height of their power and always right, as if the native's voices were unheard.

The indigenous people of Crete tried to gratify the Greeks by constructing pagan temples. They had accepted the foreign gods of the intruders out of an act of survival.

Raphael urged the natives and settlers alike to convert and follow righteous customs of the seventh heavens. He implored the immigrants to abstain from behavior that led to orgies of slaughter and inhumane treatment of helpless victims.

The settlers were only concerned about idol worship and sacrificing to gods of the fifth heavens.

Raphael and Lilith exalted the Creator and the blessings He had given them. The gate was temporarily open for the colonizers and natives alike to accept the faith of the seventh heavens. The grace period was slowly ticking away.

He warned them faith without action is dead. There was no alternative but to ask the Creator to forgive their past sins. The Creator had commanded the seventh heavens to stand back and allow the settlers to shed their hunger for greed and power as if they were newborns.

These new settlers from the Balkans had destroyed the Minoans' two thousand years of history. Their unique place in society had been overshadowed by the Greeks, who had gained access to their glorious achievements.

Across the Mediterranean, many Afro-Asiatic natives found refuge in the slopes of Africa's mountains. Meanwhile, the Greeks were rampaging towards Egypt, seeking to loot everything of value.

In the midst of the chaos, soldiers banded together with other Afrocentric nations to fight against the European takeover, hoping to put an end to their dominance. The hatred between these groups knew no bounds, for the settlers had created a caste system that divided the Mediterranean, leaving an indelible mark that could never be undone. This invisible caste loomed over them like a predator, relentlessly seeking to rule over all. In the face of such primitive forces, there was no escape from the inevitable battle for control.

The culture of the Cretans was destroyed mercilessly, and nothing could be done about it. The carnage became the social norm, as though the old culture of the Minoans was frozen in time.

Some wandered in the rocky plains of the Arabian Desert, with each tribe living as individual units governed by a single authoritative chief. There was no peace or quiet from the savage invaders, only continuous starvation. The migration came with furious hatred. The evil gods had no mercy, traveling unseen. The natives had no cure for the wicked plague as their freedom slipped away.

The wandering tribes became suspicious of all strangers. Still, they sometimes adopted the polytheistic gods of the fifth heavens instead of their ancestral, omnipotent Creator of the seventh heavens, who demanded absolute loyalty. The fifth heavens asked that they worship the pagan gods of the outer world.

The pathogen of hatred shattered the openness of the Mediterranean and unified them around ethnic and religious ideology. Tribal battles ripped the Aegean apart like the melting away of snowflakes.

The fifth heavens made a deliberate effort to erase all memories of spirituality in the Mediterranean by implanting the plague of the adversary, which spread rapidly through the Aegean like a tidal wave. This plague of hatred injected into the Aegean was a powerful tool for white settlers, which only strengthened with each victory against the natives.

Everything on the surface of the Aegean was destroyed and replaced with images that soothed the dominance of the new invaders from the Balkans. The fifth heavens became comfortable in controlling the thoughts and consciousness of the residents and even created a paradise for the new masters of the land.

In many ways, the whole world was on fire. Never had the world been on a dark path of being conquered by spiritual forces. It was a crucial moment that elevated the gods of the fifth heavens. The great tragedy was humanity had been divided for the benefit of the pagan gods. The Balkan settlers had become heroes for the pagan gods of the outer world.

The primary goal for the fifth heavens was to dominate and instill as much terror as they could. Their strategy was crucial. Communities were subjected to their power. The fury of the fifth heavens gave them a reason to be brutal. They executed citizens by hanging them from trees, incinerated homes and shops, and mercilessly lashed individuals. No one - not even the young or elderly - was spared from their torment, as they wept amid the bloodshed.

White settlers became accomplices to the malevolent entities of the fifth heavens. Some natives willingly joined in adoring these new, sinister deities from beyond. This novel form of worship introduced into the Aegean incited retribution from the seventh heavens, albeit without interfering with potential rivals of the natives. The seventh heavens endured acts of physical aggression without intervention until granted permission by the Creator.

The pyramid of power was passed on to white settlers by the fifth heavens, leaving Raphael uncertain about when the seventh heavens would step in. The streets were strewn with those who had fallen, either succumbing to a sword's downward stroke or being trampled by charging cavalry.

In no time at all, the Mediterranean found itself engulfed in chaos and transformation. The people of darker skin tones were seen as the primary foes, since the fall of the once-outcast angels. Meanwhile, a gentle breeze brushed over the shoreline, carrying images of unimaginable terror.

Yet in these challenging times, the Afrocentric people clung steadfastly to their religious values—devotion to the firstborn covenant kept them strong and determined.

However, amid religious virtues, all Afrocentric people are yoked to the firstborn covenant. Their protection and strength became ingrained in gratifying the Divine Creator of the natural world and spiritual realm of the outer world.

Interestingly enough, these Afrocentric folks embraced several aspects of Greek culture—from worshiping multiple gods for protection to living amidst the city's existing deities. As such, hidden forces from celestial realms played an unseen part in shaping the Mediterranean's ultimate fate.

Primarily, European settlers viewed territories along the Mediterranean and Nile as a part of a newfound world. They firmly believed that genetic distinctions in the Afrocentric population often indicated inferiority. The white colonizers saw an advantage in transforming the Aegean region into a powerful empire. Peace was non-existent for those opposing the rule of the fifth heavens. As long as they revered the fifth heavens, the white settlers maintained absolute authority.

In the eyes of Europeans, blackness represented a despised race of the pagan gods from the outer world. However, for Afrocentric people, it symbolized a unique lifestyle, embracing everything but paganism—unless it was forced upon them. Unfortunately, the faith of these natives was shattered by the calamity from the fifth heavens, leaving them eager to serve the creator God from the seventh heavens.

The Europeans cleverly pitted people of color against each other, attaining some success. The final, devastating blow to the vulnerable side came through a cunning divide-and-conquer tactic. The life they had known and cherished was disintegrating before their very eyes.

CHAPTER 5

Many aspects of Raphael's life forced him to face great misery and to make peace, but the presence of evil was in every direction.

His dreams became dim, and he experienced an awful feeling of regret. There was no place for peace with the modern understanding of warfare.

Raphael fled from Pergamon to Lystra. He saw black men and women marching in shackles and chains along the riverbanks.

Little children were weeping and walking alongside the adults unchained, but they were prisoners as much as their parents were.

Others seemed to be walking toward their death with the white slavers brandishing a sword. It was a painful sight. These colonizers controlled the captives' every move.

Their eyes glowed with fear as they were led to their designated place. Without hesitation, the captives were led away, filled with horror and anger but stared silently at the ground.

They understood that stepping out of line meant greater physical and mental pain. They were made cruelly aware of the pain of slavery.

The more profit and economic freedom for the European oppressors, there was sometimes little freedom for the oppressed. There was constant treachery and manipulation as the agony became more mental than physical. The slavers' voices sounded like empty words, a notion to brainwash them with a more profound sense of discipline.

Many managed to preserve their freedom by generating enough resources to appease their new rulers. Accumulating wealth and material possessions took center stage. Some even managed to buy their loved ones out of bondage, moving around with a semblance of liberty. However, it was a deceptive game, coaxing them into believing they'd risen above the less fortunate. Balkan settlers wielded political power in the region and greatly influenced daily life.

Raphael and Lilith felt utterly powerless, consumed by the fear of death. They witnessed a relentless struggle for survival at every turn. A seemingly endless journey lay before them, with the oppressive truth lurking ominously like a spider weaving its web.

In this new age, a wave of anxiety weakened the people's resolve to battle the invaders occupying the coastal islands. Yet, fear urged them only to submit to their new rulers.

Raphael saw this as the perfect opportunity to bring a message of salvation and free the people from their wrongdoings. He spoke the divine words of the Creator to defend the Aegean's sovereignty and protect its people. There was no time for delays.

He rose bravely at daybreak, gazing intently at the crimson-gold sunlight. Only Lilith, who stayed near him, knew his identity. Spreading wisdom was their task, especially after hatred had seeped through the Aegean like a poisonous plague.

Lilith chuckled softly and shook her head. She mentioned her past involvement in toppling nations and expressed amusement at humanity's divisions. "I'm grateful for a change of heart, thanks to a loving Creator," Lilith declared. "I'm eager to share the genuine message of salvation with the lost souls inhabiting this world."

The captivating Lilith led a double life, transitioning between human forms and a shimmering spiritual presence. However, she made an abrupt choice to forge a path for righteousness in a heartbeat. No longer hindered by pride or corruption, Lilith dedicated herself to embodying and promoting grace.

Her proclamation resounded powerfully, and as their conversation unfolded, they started to envision their new lives ahead. Raphael realized with unwavering certainty that they were called upon to alert others across the Mediterranean about impending threats. A surge of confidence washed over him.

A fierce storm of emotions raged within him, amid a bizarre and ghastly period. The relentless bloodshed and ruthless enforcement of obedience were pushing him to the brink of insanity. Yet, Lilith had been through unspeakable agony. Her soul now blazed with love, her pain too immense to disregard, while her thoughts clung to a long-lost vision of happiness. Raphael gazed into her eyes, sharing a moment of stillness.

Lilith's words had left him breathless in some sense. However, he remained skeptical about the purity of her loving heart. After all, she had borne witness to humanity's unholy descent from divinity, causing the loss of their earthly paradise and severing their connection with God. For ages, she dwelled in the shadows alongside avenging angels.

The thought that she could annihilate lives without love or tranquility within her soul was deeply unsettling. But now, she chose to cradle her human heart within an embrace of affection.

The Creator had granted her abundant existence on Earth and in the outer realms, which Raphael recognized as part of her life's journey. And now, it was time for them both to forge ahead.

Raphael held Lilith's shoulders, his head hanging in sadness. He gathered himself, knowing they needed to walk with determination and mindfulness to stay true to their beliefs. Together, they arrived in a city a few miles from Pergamon, where local Cretans lived amongst the new inhabitants. Many had adopted the prevalent Greek way of life.

Inside the temple, Raphael spoke passionately about the Creator's love and a divine message from the highest of heavens. Some listened intently; he urged them to abandon the false assurances of lesser celestial realms and embrace the one true Creator of all things seen and unseen. But his words were met with anger by Greeks accusing him of desecration, sparking a heated confrontation.

Raphael faced numerous obstacles and was taken aback by the devotion of the people to their local deities. The idea of an all-encompassing Creator seemed beyond their comprehension. He had assumed that they were ready for the revelation of a perfect Creator they knew so much about. Yet, they struggled to accept that the fifth heavens were subject to a higher authority.

Recognizing their perspective, Raphael knew his message was unlike anything they had ever encountered. Some came to him with amazement, seeking refuge from the chaos of hatred. With open arms, he welcomed them, and tears flowed.

The experience touched their very souls, as if they were seeing the world anew. Their faces lit up with triumph as they listened to tales of the Creator God. Overjoyed, their spirits soared free from the deception of the fifth heavens. But at the same time, it felt deeply disrespectful towards the only gods they had ever known. Regardless, they couldn't look away from Raphael.

He embodied loyalty, patience, and a unique, deeper sense of love for humankind that these people had never felt before.

As the realization dawned that this newfound reverence meant everyone was equal under the sun, skepticism grew. Life seemed too perfect for the settlers in this world governed by the fifth heavens. Yet, this fresh appreciation for humankind couldn't fill the emptiness within.

It was the love Raphael brought from the seventh heavens—a love that bound each molecule intimately and connected with Lilith's soul. It was his only known way, but the battle would be challenging. The Greeks needed to abandon their relentless quest for domination and shift to a love encompassing the Creator with all their heart and soul. That entailed a universal love for every human being. Unfortunately, a sense of bitterness cast a dark cloud directly over their hearts.

Raphael found himself battered and dragged beyond the city walls. Collapsing to his knees, he cried out to his Lord for strength as they encircled him like participants in some arcane ceremony—slowly moving while fixating their gaze upon him.

Surrounded by the crowd, Raphael attempted to regain his footing but struggled to find balance. He eventually found it by holding onto Lilith tightly.

Lilith approached the boisterous crowd, which continued to mock and shout insults at him. Undisturbed, she listened to their crude laughter, sensing the familiar malevolent energy coursing through them. They likely never embraced the concept of unity or shared a common vision.

Raphael, though shocked and overwhelmed, remained conscious enough to hear the nasty threats from the repugnant voices around him. Tears streamed down his face as he attempted to comprehend the horrific situation, struggling to breathe. It was at this moment that Lilith began to sing.

Her melodious voice brought an immediate hush over the rowdy mob. Captivated by her enchanting song, it pierced their hearts and moved some to join in with newfound fervor.

Having faced death both in heaven and on earth, Lilith was undeniably mortal, but her soul brimmed with a fresh sense of love. She no longer feared anything or sought retribution; she had transcended her past role as one of the Angels of Vengeance.

Embracing a newfound serenity, she found herself drawn away from the turmoil of the fifth heavens. Her perspective changed, choosing a life full of love, which was cherished by the Creator. Raphael rose to his feet and accompanied Lilith back to town for recovery.

He cleared the unholy image from his thoughts with a sudden quietness. In Lilith's mind, the brutal violence served as a precise trial. She tenderly turned to Raphael, wiping his face with a white cloth.

Raphael pondered over the Creator's love for a people who acted with such cruelty, intending to suppress an entire race. With every passing moment that he questioned his faith, despair contaminated his thoughts about the divine will of the Creator.

A voice urged him to endeavor in transforming the barbaric nature of humanity. Should the Creator allow it, he must return to the seventh heavens to flee this nightmare.

Violence persisted in the Mediterranean at the hands of white settlers, while questions regarding the enigmatic fifth heavens continued to grow. It seemed as though hope for improvement had vanished.

The Mediterranean landscape remained tormented by war. Every corner was dominated by towering pagan statues reaching skyward. These idols seemingly brought peace and triumph to the region; however, respite from violence continually dissolved back into chaos time and time again.

In each conquered region, Greek gods were worshipped in the same way as the ancient Aryans. Only their names were changed, adding a new astrology dimension to the Hellenistic World.

For example, Greek rites in honor of Poseidon, the Olympian god of the sea, earthquakes, floods, and drought became identified with the Hindu god of the seas and storms. The Hindu god Varuna was also associated with the rivers, water, and ocean. The pagan gods were taken to distant lands as far as the eye could see. They were conquerors, and the pagan gods were like unseen soldiers fighting together. They were yoked in the same web.

The Greeks came to believe the fifth heavens sent out weather patterns to influence individuals to help in everyday life and war. The gods of the fifth heavens were being widely integrated, appearing as wooden figures and stylishly appareled in daily lives.

The pursuit of wealth and appreciation for the arts positioned Greeks as prominent intellectual figures in politics. This enabled them to thrive as politicians, soldiers, teachers, doctors, and philosophers. Despite their reverence for the written constitution and adherence to the rule of law, Greek military conquests were brutal, resulting in ruthless expansion and bloodshed. This left little room for compassion or fairness toward the indigenous natives.

Forced into submission and silenced in daily life, the natives lost hope for a future in Greece and remained unaware of the principles of justice. A somber shadow loomed over the Aegean islands, clouding them with unceasing violence stemming from white supremacy.

Military service was essential to daily life, and their imperialistic pursuits were often achieved through pain and sacrifice instead of peace. The laws focused more on the empowerment of priesthood rather than liberty, justice, or equality, enabling them to manipulate rules to their advantage.

The Balkan settlers engaged in epic battles alongside their many gods, achieving numerous victories and learning from any defeats. For them, victory was simply not enough - they believed they possessed a divine gift bestowed upon them by the heavens above.

The favor was returned by forcing their idolatrous creed on their defeated foes. Heroic figures haunted the crossroads, with each statue regarded as a sacred ritual to the pagan gods of the outer world and cult of the dead.

The settlers rapidly spread their religious beliefs across the Mediterranean. Meanwhile, Egyptians on the opposite shore felt the pressure from the Hyksos settlers seeking power. The Hyksos arrived in Egypt on ships they had seized from the Minoans in Crete.

Facing off with these curious Euro-centric newcomers who had ties to Greece, the Egyptians aimed to protect their land in Upper Egypt. The Hyksos' goal, however, was to control trade along the Nile Delta and acquire their piece of prosperity. Though considered a lesser Balkan tribe, they eventually gained control over five significant cities in Palestine.

Reaching out to relatives and fellow tribes for support, the Hyksos enticed them with promises of free land. Consequently, this led to a massive influx of foreigners onto Egyptian soil and granted them enough strength for potent political and military influence in the region.

Years of famine left Egypt vulnerable, tilting the balance towards these ambitious settlers who sought to seize land and freedom from native Egyptians.

The bold Balkan newcomers took over Memphis and endeavored to expand their military reach southward. With an air of confidence, they marched victoriously throughout the Nile in a surprise campaign.

In the South, native Egyptians triumphantly reclaimed their independence while, in central and northern Egypt, Balkan settlers took charge with their Avaris capital at the helm. These settlers brought a priesthood that became more powerful than the Pharaohs, centered around the god Amun. As Amun gained importance, he merged with Ra, the sun god, creating Amun-Ra.

Lower Egyptians joined forces with the Cushites of Ethiopia and Nubia to reclaim control along the eastern Mediterranean Coast. White Anglo-Saxons were either expelled or enslaved in Egypt, and the nation embraced its independence. Despite this victory, the Balkan settlers received assistance from mysterious and mighty gods that cursed and haunted Egypt.

To confront these evil forces, Egypt needed to wield the divine sword of the Creator, which they had neglected. Egyptian blood became a symbol of superiority rather than a stigma. Although Greeks were expelled from Egypt, their influences on governance, war, and religion remained.

The invasion of Buhen led to its destruction and prompted a massive fortress built between Upper and Lower Egypt to safeguard trade routes. After defeating the Balkan settlers, Amun-Ra emerged as a national hero in Egyptian daily prayer.

Amun-Ra's significance and prosperity expanded across Egypt, earning the title of the king of gods. The Egyptians embraced various foreign deities from distant lands, particularly during the New Kingdom, leading to Amun-Ra evolving into Zeus Ammon, associated with ancient Greece's Zeus.

The awe-inspiring temples of Luxor on the Nile River's east bank and Madīnat Habu on the west bank showcased Egyptian devotion to Amun-Ra. As the most venerated deity, numerous pyramids throughout Egypt were constructed in his honor.

In this ancient civilization, the priesthood eventually surpassed the pharaoh in authority. Military victories were attributed to Amun-Ra's concealed influence. Thebes, renowned as "City of Amun," transformed from a humble village during the Old Kingdom era to a bustling trade hub and intellectual powerhouse during the New Kingdom period, serving as the capital of a united Egypt.

Thebes, known to the Greeks as the "City of Zeus," was a thriving cultural hub. Its main temple, Karnak, stood proudly on the city's northeastern bank. As Egyptian culture spread, individuals from Ethiopia, Nubia, and Canaan assimilated and even took up bureaucratic roles in society. Royal bloodlines were zealously guarded through marriage within families.

Amun-Ra, believed to be the creator of gods and father to all pharaohs, rose in prominence. As the gods of the fifth heavens journeyed across the Mediterranean, Egypt shifted its worship from the Sole Creator to the pagan gods of the outer world. Amun-Ra emerged as Thebes' supreme deity, while Greek religious influence expanded worldwide.

This shift in faith fostered national unity among Egyptians who attributed their fruitful land and prosperity to divine blessings. The same deities that governed Greece were now gracing Egypt with their favor.

A new chapter unfolded in Egypt's history, and word of their embrace of paganism reached Raphael in Lystra. It seemed inconceivable that Egypt had yielded so far as to construct a Greek temple for Zeus-Amun—a mortal god made of mud and mortar. And yet, with their very own hands, Egyptians constructed the Oracle of Amun in Siwa.

In a covenant nation, considering something as the highest form of blasphemy was no small matter. On Aghurmi's hill, the temple soared as a testament to that belief. Egypt, chosen by the Creator as a sanctuary for the covenant people, flourished like an earthly paradise, outshining all other civilizations. In the Old Kingdom era, Egyptians shared their faith in Yahweh and even spoke the same language as the Israelites.

However, the shift from worshiping the Creator God to embracing Amun-Ra was part of the deceitful plan hatched by the beings of the fifth heaven. Their false prosperity couldn't last, and soon a deadly plague descended upon Egypt—the likes of which had never been experienced before. This sinister curse marked the start of a slow demise for both Egyptians and Israelites, who shared common enemies and became victims of this plot orchestrated by their celestial foes.

The masses believed these foreign gods had come to Egypt to offer protection and foster progress. But instead of good fortune, a malicious curse took hold. The people's faith in these so-called blessings waned as they realized they had been deceived.

Raphael's anger simmered beneath the surface. He was certain that true blessings came directly from the Creator, not from these treacherous gods. Yet despite this divine gift, the Egyptians had allowed disobedience to flourish.

The sole Creator swore in His wrath that the covenant people would lose protection from the seventh heavens and be led into darkness by the gateways of the outer world. The Hebrew-speaking people understood when the Almighty God said, "Thou shalt have no other gods."

Throughout Mesopotamia, beyond the two great rivers of the Tigris and Euphrates and along the Nile, the inhabitants were not a unified civilization but people of complex cultures.

However, the sacred land of Egypt was known to most as the cradle of civilization. They were fused by the cultivation of written scriptures and the understanding of the one omnipotent Creator.

In a strange turn, the native Egyptians turned to the fifth heavens for security. It was as if the lash of a whip stung the nation. The brutal sting brought a new governing system that catered to Egyptians.

The transition felt like a sudden whiplash across the nation, ushering in a new authority that catered to Egyptians. This dramatic reform introduced a hierarchical system that resembled Greek governance, and materialism rose to prominence as it fueled devotion to otherworldly gods. As a result, Egypt's divine blessings gradually diminished, akin to a candle burning out.

In a land of devotion, passion, and allure, harmonious art and hieroglyphics adorned the landscape, alongside rich gold and copper mines, impressive monuments, and flowing waters. Intriguing pagan statues, brought to Egypt by white settlers, became symbolic embodiments of the nation's future submission to foreign deities.

The enigmatic fifth heaven briefly utilized Egypt to further divide the African people and strengthen their assault on the Israelites and Cushitic populations scattered across Mesopotamia. As privileged members of Egyptian society, the Israelites now faced potential enslavement under the influence of the fifth heaven and the religion of Amun-Ra.

Egypt stood as the sole Afrocentric nation favored by the fifth heaven for their ambitious conquests. The Egyptians' need for the fifth heavens' pagan gods paled in comparison to how much these celestial beings required Egypt's assistance. These otherworldly deities began to infiltrate and corrupt this once-sanctified land, introducing a new wave of self-loathing. The ultimate goal: quickly dividing black Africans under pretenses of unworthy pagan gods.

Aware of the looming peril, Raphael recognized his duty to warn Ethiopia and surrounding nations against adopting these deceptive deities. Accepting such falsehoods would undermine their culture and render their sacred covenant utterly useless. The severe repercussions that awaited them came from none other than the God of Justice.

A fleeting smile crossed Raphael's face as he pondered his thoughts. A soft voice reached him as he stood with caution. "Be strong and courageous, don't fear or be dismayed by them; the Lord your God is with you, He won't fail or abandon you."

Lilith gazed at him, taking in his pristine white clothing with a belt around his waist. Her eyes remained locked on him, scanning from head to toe. His gaze didn't falter even as a groan escaped her lips. "What's our plan now?" inquired Lilith. The sound of her hissing made him hesitate before answering.

With a reassuring smile, Raphael approached and wrapped his arms around her, trying to grasp the situation. She leaned her head on his shoulder, allowing him to regain his composure while taking a deep, calming breath. Their proximity brought unexpected comfort.

At times, Raphael saw their perilous journey across the Mediterranean as an act of desperation. There was no turning back; God was in charge and there was no room for closeness at present.

Imagining the challenges and courage required for their life-altering choice wasn't easy. While holding her tight in his arms, she didn't resist the embrace. They couldn't ignore progress and had to resist the temptation for intimacy.

There was no shame in it. Raphael found himself captivated by her physical presence, with thoughts of affection consuming him entirely.

The tender kisses and warmth shared between them ignited a fire inside; his heart raced at the mere thought of her, while butterflies filled his stomach whenever they were near. Lilith invigorated him, making him yearn to remain in her presence forever, basking in the tranquility it brought.

As Raphael wrapped his arms around her, he struggled to form coherent thoughts. Her eyes brimmed with tears while her smile shone through. Their shared connection made them feel truly alive, overcoming each struggle together as their emotions swirled.

Raphael turned away to hide his own tear-filled eyes, feeling the weight of heavy droplets on his cheeks. Gaining control of his emotions, he knew they must face whatever uncertainties the future may hold and focus on the challenges that awaited them.

He stepped back while Lilith straightened her clothes. Both were uncertain about what had occurred and shook off lingering intimate thoughts. Silently staring at one another, Raphael finally spoke: "It's time to move forward with our mission."

Their duty was clear – they had been chosen to warn both the Hebrews and God-fearing Greeks of the need to worship the Creator in the seventh heavens. This divine task was theirs to uphold.

Wiping away his tears, Raphael recognized that the pain within his heart mirrored a deeper truth – this sense of unease and emptiness resonated with the Creator's own disappointment at humanity's moral failings.

CHAPTER 6

Raphael and Lilith set off toward coastal waters after a brief fasting period. Embarking on a captivating voyage, they cruised amidst the picturesque Greek islands, navigating the rugged hills and scenic valleys along the Mediterranean coastlines. With an air of excitement, they continued on to the mesmerizing shallow waters near the alluring North African shoreline.

Raphael caught a glimpse of Lilith, who had succumbed to her fatigue and fallen asleep. He cherished these stolen glances. Her energy had depleted, and sleep overtook her. Raphael allowed himself to close his eyes, relishing the soothing sway of the waves against the ship. Submerged in a profound slumber, the rhythm of the water rocking back and forth set him at ease. Together, they slept as the vessel persisted through the tumultuous ocean.

Then, a subtle, continuous sound emerged from the vessel's side. Trying to disregard the nagging vibration, he shifted his face away. But his curiosity won out; his eyes flitted open as he sprang to his feet and swiftly approached the ship's porthole. Peering through the circular opening, he observed colossal waves rising from deep below the sea's surface.

The powerful sea engulfed the surroundings, its intensity and spray captivating him. The scene felt strange. Edging closer to Lilith, he noticed she was sound asleep. The wind's howl amplified, its vigor growing by the second. Titanic waves swelled, water flooding the vessel, making his heart pound at the sight of their enormity. Amongst the waves, something caught his attention.

Raphael hesitated but knew he had to wake Lilith. An unknown entity appeared to ride the waves, approaching their vessel. Although he just awoke from a dream, anxiety still gripped him. The water receded quickly, settling at its usual depth.

He held his breath as the wind nudged the vessel with another sequence of mighty waves. The moon cast a brilliant glow while distant thunder murmured, and lightning blazed like a fiery lamp.

Once more, the tumultuous waves rumbled, and a surge swelled upward to meet the deck. Raphael gazed across the expansive ocean and its haunting commotion of wind and waves. He stood transfixed by the terrifying sight of ferocious waves crashing against one another while fear crept upon him as they closed in.

The ship shuddered under the relentless pounding of waves against its hull. The immense surge forced the vessel to sway and bounce, helpless to resist its dominating power.

The strong current flowed violently downstream and continued to plague the sea with a constant, rumbling gust. The wind blew through the African sky most frighteningly. Too much water rushed onboard, and waves splashed in every direction. The sound of the wind seemed to come alive. He ran over, shaking Lilith as the waves surged onto the lower deck.

Lilith was startled and glared at him momentarily without saying a word. The ship sailed against the wind toward the horizon. Lilith caught her breath, and the panic diminished.

They paused momentarily before fleeing to the upper deck for safety. Lilith said, "It feels like demonic spirits are riding the waves." Some began to scream like little children. Raphael shouted, "Come up here," as passengers rushed up the stairs. Raphael stared down the staircase as his body twisted around, and pushing for safety.

The waves grew more powerful by the moment. There were no words to describe the awful moments of fear. Terror and the surging of the waves surrounded them.

The dynamic water altered the movement of the ship. The vessel began to rock as the ship wildly fought against the wind.

As soon as they settled down again, a seismic disruption cracked the bulkhead of the vessel. The pressure from the eruption blew a deep cavity in the ship. Water rushed in from the floor.

For a moment, the crew managed to navigate the twist of the waves, but the wind shifted to the northwest of the vessel, and the night skies soared into darkness. The mission was in grave danger.

Above the waves, fiery flames rose slowly in the bright light of the blue sky. The captain steered the ship against the force of the current. The ship bounced back and forth and rocked side to side through the ripples of the water.

The pressure sent hot steam flowing throughout the ship. Black smoke filled the sky, followed by streaks of stars dashing like thunderbolts of lightning. The immense fireballs conquered the darkness, brightening up the night sky. There were flames everywhere.

The scene was disastrous! The ship lay in pieces, its blood-filled remains swallowed by the darkness. Fire and smoke billowed from the debris, reminiscent of a battlefield. Battling against winds, waves, and floating wreckage, the survivors were unexpectedly thrust into their worst nightmare: braving the unforgiving depths of the ocean.

As suffocating smoke filled the air, lifeless bodies littered the site. Terror and grief intermingled with cries for help as crew members wailed, their blood painting a horrifying picture. The clamor of destruction echoed like thunderous drums.

The cries and yells of agony filled the air around the shipwreck, as though bearing the wrath of a vengeful death's curse. The once serene ocean morphed into a watery tomb taking hold of the doomed ship in its expansive grip. Relentlessly rising waves filled the inky night — escape seemed impossible.

Amidst chaos, someone shouted, "God help me! Please, Lord!" Shipwrecked passengers were trapped in a living hell with no savior in sight. Panic spread rapidly alongside dwindling hope.

Eventually, the vessel succumbed to its watery grave; billows of smoke shrouded remnants of nightlights within. More dead than alive; debris piled upon helpless victims like a demonic war against humanity.

A shadow loomed over the water—clouds giving way to another ship engulfed by a bitter wind gust. Despite fear gripping every heart, the colossal cargo ship could take all passengers aboard. Ocean waves roared as they tore through burning wreckage.

Voices cried out to stay above water: "Oh my God!" Families ripped apart; children and other survivors attempted to evade flames that danced on turbulent waters.

Frantic splashes filled the air as hundreds pushing and shoving, making their way toward the ship's entrance. As chaos swirled around the new ship, desperate pleas for help rang out: "Please help us!" Raphael joined the fray and assisted others on deck, their desperation palpable.

He wanted to help whoever was in need of assistance from the shipwreck. Lilith hadn't joined the survivors, and Raphael knew he had to return to look for her.

He was in pain, but the cries motivated him to push forward. Raphael was still hoping to capture a glimpse of Lilith beyond the waves. His thoughts were bitter as if time kept repeating itself.

Tears filled his eyes, making him unable to see through the thick fog. Shouts from the crowd continued with the recurring sounds of gasps for air. The fog was so heavy, with very little visibility. Nothing would ever be the same without Lilith. He wondered what might have happened to her.

Lilith was lost in the water, and no one seemed to know how many passengers had survived the horrible ordeal.

While the crowd climbed onto the ship's deck, he swam back across the water to look for Lilith. He looked among the dead and the floating bodies for her.

Raphael worked through the floating debris and the thick fog, but there was no sign of the beautiful Lilith. His mind was fixed on staying alive as he continued to help as many victims as possible.

He was determined, but Raphael soon realized it was impossible to find Lilith among so many dead bodies.

Corpses were floating and curling through the water. Raphael swam toward the helpless bodies in search of the survivors crying out. He knew he didn't have much time left to save the injured.

People were screaming, crying, and swimming for safety, trying to get away from moving debris.

In the shadowy night, Raphael's search for Lilith persisted, his heart pounding with fear that any lifeless body he stumbled upon might be hers. With every thought of her, his anxiety escalated. He couldn't fathom a world without her - it would feel hollow and incomplete. As they had faced so much together, he'd imagined their new beginnings entwined as one. With urgency, Raphael raced back to the ship to board.

Soon enough, the ship captain ordered the survivors to be taken down below deck and forcefully separated before lodging.

Once on board, the men, women, and children were chained and crammed at the bottom of the ship, where the cargo was kept. The cargo hold was turned into horrible living quarters on the way toward Egypt. The sailors treated them with contempt. There was no sympathy to be found.

It was a difficult and terrifying journey. Something was wrong. It made no sense for a rescue to turn into horror.

This ship's crew had found abundant casualties to be enslaved while on their journey to Egypt and Israel. The ship was a relief vessel of Greek origin heading to Egypt to assist the Balkan settlers, in a fight to take over the region.

The crew, motivated by greed, had very little compassion. Anyone with a black or brown face was considered an enemy to the gods of the fifth heavens, with no exception. Colorism and the Eurocentric caste structure were wildly alive.

The air was filled with a mad sense of envy brought down from the hills of the Balkans. It was a silent rivalry that pierced the Mediterranean.

Raphael's every move seemed to bring pain and sorrow in a world he had no control over. He became helpless with an empty spirit that yearned for peace and understanding. It seemed that he had failed. His heartbeat raced out of control. His entire body ached with pain, and the nightmares never ceased.

Instead, anger surged through his soul with a sinister desire like a powerless creature frozen in time.

He lay awake at night, kicking and whacking against the chains. The iron seemed to mock his sadness. His bruises and lashes from the whips were for rebelliousness. Many were whipped into silence or faced death by the whip's repeated strokes.

In the fierce heat of the day, prisoners were tied together and forced to bow their heads in prayer to praise the gods of the fifth heavens while their legs were shackled down to the ship's deck. Raphael tried to focus his vision, but the groans of the dying wouldn't allow him peace. The captives sobbed and groaned as their dignity and liberty vanished.

A growing unease permeated the dungeon's living quarters, where compliance and allegiance were maintained by the sting of the whip. They couldn't fathom the heinous crime they had committed to warrant such brutality.

Raphael struggled with the challenging task of confronting his own identity, a feat the deities of the outer realm sought to sabotage. These pagan gods aimed to make him feel insignificant and inhuman. As his thoughts raced along with the harsh injustices he faced, time seemed to slip away before he could grasp the full situation. In truth, Raphael fit the stereotype of an enslaved individual from the oppressors' perspective, or according to the white man's viewpoint. His dark complexion, shining brown eyes, wide shoulders, and strong physique met those cruel expectations.

No one could have guessed that Raphael was actually an angel disguised as a human. He had to adapt to the rhythm of his earthly constraints. Living in dark-skinned human form during those times meant he faced discrimination and was treated as inferior. A person's worth hinged on the fortune they brought to their oppressors.

Each word he uttered reflected the power and vulnerability of the fifth heaven in his life's mission, not by silence or fear, but through the continuous acknowledgement of the awe-inspiring Creator who governed the rise and fall of the sun. Despite this, his warnings and prophetic visions were largely dismissed.

From the moment he came to earth, Raphael's mission was to expose the spiritual world of the fifth heavens, regardless of the penalty he might endure. He chose to embrace the pain of the dungeon and the physical deaths all around him with a stoic resolve.

The slave ship reached its destination in Egypt to change detained passengers at the dock. The ship's next stop was Israel. The iron collar was unattached from the neck of each confined person, and they were marched down the passageway with the heavy bull chain still connected to each prisoner's ankles.

The prisoners were bound by waist chains that pierced their skin, connecting to leg irons with a longer chain, effectively preventing any attempts at escape or running. The handcuffs, locked twice, were either fastened to a leather belt or to the waist chain itself. Shackled in this manner, they were sold to the highest bidder.

Subjected to unimaginable cruelty, these individuals were engulfed in shame and self-loathing. They faced daily mental reinforcement of their perceived inferiority—a message which suggested that darker skin made them less valuable. This insidious mistreatment instilled a deep-rooted fear that subconsciously steered their minds towards believing they were truly lesser beings.

All of a sudden, a chilling mixture of dread and panic filled the air as the echo of rattling chains and labored breaths emerged from the dungeon. The captives' trembling voices signaled the devastating beginning of their end.

As Raphael left the ship, he spotted Lilith, bound by leg irons. Their eyes locked for an instant before he was shoved forward by a slave trader. They shared a brief nod, but their tear-filled eyes revealed the overwhelming anguish they endured.

Despite it all, seeing Lilith alive brought tears of relief and a smile to Raphael's face. He struggled to control his emotions and swayed from side to side as he approached the ship's entrance.

In the suffocating confines of the dungeon, he stumbled unwillingly towards his fate - being sold to the highest bidder, enslaved by a nightmarish system of corruption. This was the grim reality of life in a world under the iron grip of the fifth heaven.

In Egypt, a unique bond formed with their Egyptians relatives, who saw their wartime triumphs as divine gifts from the celestial gods of the fifth heavens. This fresh polytheistic belief system bolstered Egyptian patriotism, leading them to view neighboring people around the Mediterranean and Nile as lesser rivals. This mindset was a remnant from white settlers.

The Egyptians believed they were the chosen ones, and their actions could either anger or please the gods of the universe. Though the Balkan settlers were vanquished physically, they claimed a spiritual victory by weaving Greek mythology into Egyptian traditions.

The Egyptians enjoyed their prosperity but had become major players in this epic drama of a new world order in which the gods of the fifth heavens ruled by perpetrating vengeance as ruthlessly as possible. The Egyptians established a social structure based on rules from the fifth heavens, which spread throughout the region.

Soon, the spark of an intricate system thwarted the Hamites, Semitics, and Israelites into idolatry. The elevation of Egypt lifted the pagan gods of the fifth heavens to dominance in the region.

The Egyptians forced the defeated settlers down toward Canaan or ancient Israel, causing a bitter rivalry for control of the economy. Not too long afterward, the custom and religion of the settlers became the norm in Canaan.

In the valley of Gehenna in Jerusalem, some parents sacrificed their firstborn children by placing them in a fiery inferno that contained altars dedicated to the gods of the fifth heavens.

The territory of Canaan fell into the hands of Eurocentric domination, and a new world order of elitism spread like wildfire across the Mediterranean.

The new settlers possessed superior weapons of iron as well as horse-driven chariots that enabled the conquerors to master the land and force the natives into servitude.

The establishment of colorism became the norm, and a caste system was alive in the new territory. It was a well-thought-out plan by migrants from the Balkans, and the gods of the outer world became the dominant power.

The rules were relatively simple for the settlers but torture for the natives. If a person had black skin, they were detained and subjugated to corporal punishment when they didn't surrender to authority.

The captives were then introduced to the essence of slavery to uplift the lifestyle of the white settlers by any means necessary.

CHAPTER 7

THE MAKESHIFT DUNGEON WHERE Lilith and the other women were kept was at the bottom of the stairwell and used to carry out some of the deadliest atrocities.

It was hell with iron fixtures, painted pipes, and foul odors from years of unsanitary leakages. The women had to find a way out of this deep, dark hole.

The dungeon was some hell on earth—a place plagued with continued rape and the shackles of physical and mental slavery. The doors were locked for those who suffered the misfortune of entering this hellhole. The dungeon lay deep within the ship's inner stomach below the surface.

The guards never pretended to be friendly and were ready to kill or punish the captives for any reason that fit their ego.

It was a terrible place and the end of life for many caught up in the wicked snare of the fifth heavens. There was no fresh air. The motive was always to produce as much labor as possible to allow the captives to be bought or sold.

The women's lives had been turned inside out, and they'd been violated and abused without the fear of justice.

They were locked in the dungeon—a meaningless life that wasn't decent enough to be lived. Any loud noise or the opening and slamming of the dungeon doors made the women nervous about impending abuse.

The women seemed entirely abandoned by the seventh heavens and all who believed in morality.

The slavers didn't adhere to any just or ethical system at all. The young ladies were sobbing and crying out heavy tears. Lilith silently watched as her face burned with anger. She could taste the bitterness in the air. The anger seared her soul with the promise of vengeance.

The captives were powerless, and the Balkan settlers had achieved authority. The women were forced to do whatever satisfied their abductors. Some women cried out to the white slavers for compassion, but their voices were ignored.

The slavers recognized the dominance of the fifth heavens and saw the gods as their guardians, as long as the seventh heavens remained uninvolved in the conflict. It was typical for them to either align with a side of the cosmic order or disappear into nothingness.

In the dungeon, the women became frantic. Lilith's eyes welled up with tears as she closed them and started singing soothing tunes to drown out the sorrowful atmosphere of their prison.

The dungeon was a terrible, burdensome place filled with immense sorrow, as though the weight of the world pressed down upon their shoulders. A constant sense of despair colored their lives in captivity.

As Lilith heard footsteps approaching, she could make out faint voices and found the scent of cigars growing more powerful. She observed the slavers engaging in reprehensible acts every day, always sporting the same wicked grin on their faces.

One sailor walked past her, and she looked at him in awe. The sailor strolled, then turned and stared at Lilith before changing direction. The sailor went further to the back of the ship's dungeon.

A pale man entered the dimly-lit dungeon, the scent of his cigar intertwining with his pungent presence. His eyes held a devilish emptiness, as if untouched by sunlight, his face appeared unnaturally pale. This man was aged and rugged, his short temper evident as he gestured abruptly towards the women.

Lilith refused to look at him, keeping her head and eyes straight toward the deck. Lilith couldn't look at his pale face without quivering. The guards were unpredictable. They were constantly on guard in the makeshift dungeon on a mission to spread their pagan belief practices and graven idolatry images as much as possible.

The sole objective was to spread supremacy and ensure they understood that the white settlers were in control.

The white slavers held immense power, feeling as though they controlled life and death. With no warning, they could unleash brutal force for any reason they saw fit. It was a heartbreaking reality! Restraint was non-existent, and physical violence could be inflicted on a whim.

The pale man ran his hand through the thickness of Lilith's hair with his face so close she could feel the hot ashes from his cigar. His shirt was soaked with sweat as he blew a puff of smoke that swirled in midair, filling the air with an unpleasant aroma. She could see how much he enjoyed his gnawing devilish acts with his high-pitched laughter. The slavers could turn from unashamed lust to murder in an instant. There was no escaping the intrinsic mischief of the fifth heavens.

There was an evil spirit in the hearts of these wild men without the faintest trace of remorse. The women had to live amid despicable horror. All around them was pain and screaming, but no one would heed their pleas.

The endless journey heading toward Canaan was like a pipeline waiting to explode. The tension sent shivers through their bodies as the rage increased with every moment spent in the dungeon.

They wept and moaned, unable to see the sunset or the illuminating blue sky. Terror and misery permeated the dungeon from the wicked spirits in the darkness of night.

Even in sleep, there was no escape as their dreams turned into evil, twisted sorrows. There was a hunger for comfort and an unfamiliar shame for being alive. The young women didn't want to dream anymore for fear of being traumatized.

There was a little girl, delicate and pure, with the perfect beauty of youth. She appeared flawless. She couldn't comprehend why her life had disintegrated into unbearable suffering. Tears cascaded down her dark brown cheeks, as she lost all faith in ever finding happiness again.

A sailor came toward her. He reached for the young girl and urged her to be silent. She had no energy to fight back and forced herself to remain calm. His wishes were clear.

The young girl could no longer weep tears of fear and couldn't convince the white slavers to feel her pain. She could hardly breathe of being filled with grief.

There was no sympathy and nothing less than diabolical fear. Nothing was so sinister, but she lacked the strength to combat grown men with evil rage. It was like a slow death amid a cruel dream.

In a moment, she experienced a surge of tense emotion, looking into the face of a devil in absolute torture.

The slave trader's expression lit up with enthusiasm, and his tone heightened. "Are you afraid, young girl? I like the sweet taste of youth."

A smug grin stretched across his face while Lilith did her best to disregard his malicious audacity. Unfazed, he continued to display his eccentric attitude as if it were a testament to his power.

Overwhelmed with shame, the little girl hung her head low, gripped by dread and sorrow. She gazed at him in a detached manner, as if attempting to wake up from a terrible nightmare.

The little girl tried to apologize for her attractiveness, which turned the European slaver into a monster of a person. She was helpless, and it became clear that the sailors fully controlled her young body. The man still had a grin on his face.

The girl looked around nervously, but no one came to her aid. The guard cleared his throat, bringing him more confidence.

The sailor unshackled her and thrust her naked body to the back of the ship in a vacant room. Intimacy forced the girl to go from childhood to womanhood.

A tear slipped from Lilith's eyes, wishing she could prevent the harsh treatment carried out by the sailor. But she was chained and helpless. Her soul boiled with a feverish emotion. She inhaled deeply with fresh tears shimmering in her eyes. The sailor enjoyed his evil deeds with great satisfaction.

Lilith closed her eyes tightly. She could hear the girl calling for compassion. The pleading in the girl's voice was still in the corner of her mind. Lilith's head tilted from side to side without saying a word. She could not reach out to help. She shook her head, trying to block out the sound.

The young girl had been selected by somebody with a glimpse of power who needed to show his superiority. The horrible turmoil of cowardice continued.

Immediately, the young girl's dreams would be forever altered by the desires that rendered her inhuman yet human enough for his satisfaction. She couldn't unravel the thoughts that were piercing her soul.

The sailor's fantasy came true that night, and the girl's darkest fear became a reality. The women were stuck inside a nightmare.

The ship was paradise for the sailors in a hierarchy of power combining wealth, sexual satisfaction, and authority over life and death.

The dungeon remained silent for a moment. The women seemed to have lost the will to live. The downpour of iniquity continued.

Anyone who set out to resist the white man's way of life would find themselves at the bottom of the sea. Liberty, economic freedom, or happiness was not meant for people of African heritage in this new age of Eurocentric conquest.

Pleasure for the tyrants was the consequence of being dark and pretty. Being white was the standard of superiority that brought a sense of satisfaction and economic freedom. The atmosphere on board the ship was gruesome. The panic set in.

It was becoming increasingly complex for Lilith to stomach the sickness, but she was defenseless. The girls were too young to fight these savages. They were caught in the snare of dominance.

The barbs burrow deep into their very essence. Lilith, for the time being, could only unleash her cutting remarks as a verbal warning.

There was a lot of cruelty at the hands of the slavers, and strange circumstances led to the women being taken hostage on this long voyage of torture.

Tears streamed down Lilith's face, her heart aching as if pierced by an arrow. The pain grew more intense, consuming her until she grasped her own helplessness. Thoughts of escape shriveled to nothingness, leaving her trapped in her own despair.

Lilith's fiery words only brought more discipline from their white captors, resulting in an atmosphere of relentless fear. The guard glanced at Lilith, smirking maliciously. She took a deep breath, her expression shifting from shock to tranquility as she closed her eyes.

Aware that death could befall any or all of them in an instant, Lilith knew even the slightest disrespect towards the white men could lead to being cast overboard. It was crucial not to challenge their dominance, as they were like deities among them.

In a menacing tone, Lilith confronted the sailor, only to be abruptly silenced by a harsh slap from the pale-faced man puffing on a cigar. The ruthless slavers had no qualms about brutally beating or whipping the women to the brink of death. Blood trickled down her face, staining her clothes. The pale-faced man delivered another fierce blow to her chest, ordering her to keep quiet as he angrily strode away.

The slavers would never waste a moment watching the victims bleed like wild animals trapped in cages. There was no relief in sight. The plan was simple. There was less pain in being submissive. Talk only when told to do so.

The terrifying scene unfolded as the captors instilled fear into their victims. Overwhelmed by their emotions, the slavers made the women question whether they would live through this nightmarish experience.

The women remained shackled in the dungeon daily, looking at faces with the same insane rage. It was a time they wanted to forget, but the metal band shackled to their ankles and wrist would never allow them. There were no words to express the pain.

They would hear noises throughout the night, and the rotation of the vessel became perfectly normal. The women were so caught up in fear that being clung together in chains became a delusion within their dreams.

They prayed things would be better and tried to ignore the bitterness that haunted them like a vicious cloud. There was no denying the torment and the evil that fell on them like a cold winter storm.

How could anyone be so wicked? It seemed every slaver had an evil spirit without the fear of God. There were so many bad memories. They were unfazed by the blood-soaked dungeon and were immune to any twisted thought of decency. Their lives had no purpose and importance, and even the idea of death clung with uncertainty. This injustice was deeply embedded in the fabric of white supremacy and Eurocentric domination. The women had never experienced anything like this. The treatment was radical, and the madness was more than exhaustion.

Lilith had done everything she could to eliminate the terror against the young women. She could feel the rage as if a fire were burning within her soul. The pain was too much to keep the teardrops from rolling down her face.

In a way, the inhumane treatment made her come alive with a passionate desire for vengeance. She closed her eyes and listened to her every thought. Her mind had altered into pure insanity. She struggled to hold on to reality.

The world had become a sad place where bloodthirsty and cowardly were elevated to supremacy. Their blackness was the only thing needed to justify the pain and suffering. The atrocities were perfectly normal, like night and day.

The evil deeds flowed like molten metal, with acts of privilege running through their veins.

The young children were no longer considered individuals with parents. They were enslaved children who could be sold to satisfy any white person willing to pay the price.

The New World absorbed whatever personal feelings the sailors had in their hearts. The new sense of dominance made the invaders absolute rulers of the new territory around the Aegean Sea. White privilege had made them forget that they were human.

Every bit of sanity was overshadowed by constant threats of punishment, rape, or right-out murder to the satisfaction of the fifth heavens. Power and control were essential for the fifth heavens and the white settlers to remain dominant.

No one would dispute the cruelty the young girls faced. They were like pieces of merchandise left waiting on shelves to be purchased by the highest bidders. The white man's ego came at the enslaved people's expense. They were forced to an eternal life of servitude to please the white man's thoughts and desires.

The ship's dungeon became a death trap, and the victims were treated like wild beasts in shackles.

To be obedient was not enough. The sudden twist of submission was just a script for imperialism. The consequences for disobeying orders given by the new rulers were horrendous.

It seemed as if a divine plan from the heavens had emerged, leading noble savages to establish a relentless system for worldwide domination. With Eurocentrism dictating their path, they were determined to bulldoze any obstacle in their pursuit of power, regardless of its impact on men, women, or children.

Lilith took a deep breath as her fears disappeared with a renewed spirit. All of a sudden, she seemed to become comfortable in her faith. Her mind became clear.

The long-suffering strangely strengthened her. She handled the grief like a silent miracle but wept heavy tears.

The women were indoctrinated into a culture of violence, self-hatred, and a sense of a god that blessed the white man in every way possible. The white men were dominant in a world where the fifth heavens had such superior power. This could never be understood in the usual sense, only a branch for the white man to share power with the fifth heaven.

What is more, important than hatred against the natives was absolute power. Being submissive didn't stand a chance with the white settlers. They wanted the ability to turn the natives against each other, enough for self-hatred to thrive within their souls.

Lilith knew the Creator, who held the whole Earth in the gentle palm of His hand. He was the God of Justice. Lilith refused to live a shackled life of fear and cruel bondage. She would rather die than accept servitude.

She once lived in the seventh heavens and could go to and from the fifth heavens before being cast down as an earthly angel. She still knew the eternal God reigned high above the seventh heavens and sought to free Earth from the evil inflicted upon humankind. They prayed day and night.

She could hear the laughter in the sailors' voices, and she felt her renewed profound ability could happen at any moment. The idea of her DNA being altered back to her original state revealed a sense of freedom. Lilith wanted the Creator to hear her plea and set her free. Her prayer left no room for doubt and swift deliverance from bondage. She stood firm with a glimmer of hope. She promised that she would not walk away from her mission.

She heard the pleading in the voices of the young girls while she wiggled her body out of the shackles. The Creator gave her strength. Her prayer was answered. Lilith was rewarded freedom from the chains to live a mission of deliverance.

She managed to slip out of the leg iron at her ankles. She wiggled her feet and felt the flow of fresh, warm blood fill her body. The loosening of the shackle was terrific, the feeling of candor as the tears rolled down her face. There was no fighting the tears away while a sweet taste of revenge entered her mind.

Everything changed! It was like magic. But it was no magic at all. It was the grace of the Creator. She had a new profound energy. She drew a deep breath. In a gentle voice, she said, "Thank you, Lord! Thank you!" One of the sailors turned his head in the direction of the strange sounds, but temptation and lust kept him busy enough for Lilith to escape the shackles.

For the moment, the sailors were nowhere to be seen. The dungeon was quiet. The sailors had disappeared into the vacant rooms. Shortly one of the sailors exited the room with his bold appearance.

The women were unaware of Lilith's ability. She nodded to them to remain silent while she held her breath. Her eyes were filled with tears. She smiled with a bit of sadness toward the shackled women. A gloom of darkness lingered over her.

Lilith leaped to her feet with an unwavering heartbeat. She ran directly toward the sword the young, horny sailor laid down. He never heard her footsteps. She vanished from her body and reappeared in spiritual form, becoming invisible instantly.

She was a headless figure approaching the guard with a falchion sword. His eyes blazed with fear when he saw the waving sword coming.

The headless figure made him feel overpowered. The figure made a sudden stop before reaching the sailor. He sensed that he had been outsmarted.

She vanished into thin air. He thought his eyes were playing tricks on him. He tried to run but was quickly caught by the sword's fast movement. The young sailor cried out one last time. She grasped him momentarily before piercing the sword's blade through his body.

Lilith moved swiftly, looking for the other slaver who'd come down to the dungeon, never faltering when she shifted into her physical, visible state. She shared hardly a word, walking silently down the aisle with extraordinary inner strength.

The women shed tears, but Lilith held a finger across her lips to call for complete silence. There was not even a whisper as the girls silently watched her every footstep. They continued to wait with their worst fears while Lilith moved in stealthy silence.

They didn't have time to think, but Lilith's escape from the shackles shaped a loyalty to each other. Lilith continued through the dungeon like a ghostly shadow. There was nothing that she wanted to say, clutching the sword tightly.

Cautiously, she walked down the hallway looking for any white face that would be distracted enough for her to surprise him. She wanted badly to see the fear in the eyes of the sailors. She walked silently toward the back of the ship with her eyes focused on any sense of movement. She licked her lips, tasting revenge in the air.

The smell of cigars caught her attention. Her nose sniveled from the bitter aroma of the smoke. The slaver who'd taken the young girl was smoking again, the stench lingering throughout the dungeon. Tears surged in her eyes as she waited in a bit of anguish.

There was a pain of revenge that overshadowed her. She was no Raphael but an angel of vengeance. However, the warning to the sailors came before her ability to transition from physical to a radiant spirit of light.

Now, Judgment had come to the sailors in the form of retribution. He exited his room and confronted Lilith for being out of her chains.

Their eyes met in an instant. He looked stunned. But this time, the sailor wasn't smiling. Lilith wanted no part of a conversation but to take away his ego with death. There's no salvation at the time of Judgment. Her countless nightmares of revenge had finally come true.

The sailor appeared angry. Lilith had startled him. She stared right at him and gave him a devious smile. His soul couldn't be helped as tears dripped from the eyes of Lilith. Still, the sailor looked deep into her eyes, glancing at the other women from a distance.

"Why aren't you shackled?" The pale-faced man asked. Lilith didn't say a word. There was nothing to explain. He still shook his finger at her as she stood there in silence.

The first thing he'd thought of when he approached Lilith was fear. Then he stood there as if he'd seen a ghost in its purest form.

There was no force, only threatened words from the sailor. Lilith had turned the tide with a glimpse of hope for the shackled women. They stared straight ahead with the essence of courage. Her dark eyes fluttered with tears.

The man walked toward her, waving his filthy finger drunkenly as he cleared the smoke from his throat. He was shaking his finger like scolding a little child. His heart was beating in a sudden panic.

He held his hand toward Lilith and pointed viciously to guide her back toward the chained woman. She hesitated for a moment, glancing back toward the women in shackles. He kept waving his fingers for her to get back into her iron restraints. She shook her head and refused his command, her dark eyes staring at him through tears.

She began stepping quietly and slowly backward. He was confused by her movements. She wanted to put as much fear in him as possible. Then she made a sudden stop and lunged toward the pale-faced man. His boldness faded away. But this time, he didn't move toward her. There were few words to say.

His eyes grew wider with fear as a woman dominated him for the first time in his life. The man was astounded that Lilith had gotten out of her chains and was so threatening. All at once, he was filled with doubt.

Again, she vanished from her physical body. She changed to spirit form right before his eyes. He was dazed and filled with suspicion. The pale-faced man could no longer see her but heard her footsteps.

The man looked like he'd seen a ghost, but his ego wouldn't allow him to run. The shadowy figure struck him with paralyzing fear. He paused to glance back at the figure.

Suddenly the shadow disappeared, so the man's face swayed from left to right, his eyes wide open, searching for the figure. He paused briefly. His blood boiled with fear as he dared to challenge her in a fight.

It was as though the pale-faced man was caught in a haunting nightmare. He tried to locate Lilith's footsteps. Initially, he began to think she was imaginary, but he still stood there frozen.

There was a moment of panic as he looked around in disbelief. Lilith caught up with him as he turned his head toward the sound. She tasted blood, and the high pitch cry of the sailor gave her enormous strength.

With courage, he raised his head and gazed at the chained women. His eyes momentarily flicked back to the spot where he had last seen Lilith. Determined, he strode down the corridor, deliberately avoiding the direction of the ghost's last appearance.

Regardless of her vanishing act, the struggle must go on. Clear thinking returned to him. It was impossible for her to be unseen. He appeared to await her comeback, sensing impending danger.

He stumbled back, yet Lilith, fueled by intense emotions, pummeled him continuously. She hesitated for a moment, lost in her thoughts, before rage surged through her like a bolt of lightning. Meanwhile, the pale-faced man unsheathed his sword and stood poised, prepared to attack at the slightest hint of motion.

"It's her," he cried out, calling for reinforcements, but no one ever came to his rescue. He was scared from head to toe.

Lilith leaped into the air over the long metal blade with perfect balance, kicking him in the face and thrusting him to the deck. She paused momentarily to gather her composure or to allow him to suffer a little before killing him.

Blood poured down his pallid face, each droplet fueling the desire for vengeance. Weak and rapidly losing blood, he struggled to stand, only to collapse repeatedly. Lilith observed him intently, his eyes wide with terror. Seizing the sword, she yanked his head back by his long, dark hair. With the sword's tip pressed to the nape of his neck, she forced him to his feet, all while remaining unseen by him.

His body wracked with pain; he trembled uncontrollably as she urged him forward towards the woman. The slaver's voice shook with emotion while she guided him to face the consequences of his actions. She held her breath, listening intently to the faint whisper of terror that escaped his dying lips.

At last, the nightmare he had inflicted upon the women came to a screeching halt! She brandished the sword with a flourish before plunging it into his neck. As blood gushed from the fatal wound, her feet slid back, and his head became severed from his body.

Blood splattered onto the deck from his lifeless body in a gruesome display. The women, horrified, witnessed the entire struggle. Even with her invisibility cloak, Lilith's shadow was unmistakably visible to them.

There was a chilling sound of relief whispered throughout the ship's dungeon, yet the pain from captivity had sunk too deep into the women's minds. The pale face man's blood was all over Lilith's body as she processed what had just occurred.

Lilith was filled with rage but for a good reason. She needed to protect the women from this point forward and ease their pain from what they had experienced trapped inside the dungeon.

Lilith's fears had diminished enough to seek revenge in the death-trap of the dungeon. Any sympathy she could've had for the men faded away with the dream of freedom. Her sanity had slipped away, craving revenge. Lilith took the shackle-opener from the dead pale face man. Then she went over to the women to comfort them. She unfastened the chains and gave them their freedom.

There was no time for remorse, for all of the pain seemed to illustrate the antipathy of oppression. It was a perfect time to fight for liberty.

The women waited patiently for the other guards to enter the dungeon. They were prepared for a risky mission that would ultimately lead to freedom.

At any moment, the guards could descend into the dungeon. The women were sure the guards had heard the ruckus, yet an eerie silence prevailed. The abrupt halt of the sailor's movements was baffling, as if they were aware of the events below deck.

Apprehensively, the captives kept their eyes on the entrance, their demeanor reflecting their anxiety. They huddled beneath the staircase, straining to catch even the slightest sound while fear-filled tears welled in their eyes. They stealthily guarded the entryway.

It felt like being part of a thrilling rehearsal on stage. Their choices were to wait for the unexpected, seize the opportunity to sprint towards the upper deck as the door opened, or actively pursue their freedom through a brilliantly devised, courageous plan.

The women were rescued from the shackles but trapped in the cage of the ship's dungeon. They were freer than before but too afraid to attempt their escape. They knew nothing about what was on the other side of the dungeon's door.

The women stayed silent for a moment, trying to access their thoughts. Lilith wanted no part of fear. Then assurance flourished with the confidence of Lilith.

A prolonged rage rang out in their heads. They could taste the possibility of liberty. Whatever the consequences, the slavers would be met with brute force.

Their self-worth was diminished through senseless acts of evil valued only by the outer world of the fifth heavens. The last chance from the brutality of the dungeon had arrived.

The trail of blood from the dead slaver was sweet revenge. Despite still being confined to the dungeon, the women could savor this fleeting moment of liberation. Their days in captivity were devoid of the comforting glow of moonlight or warmth of sunlight.

They stood deep below the upper deck, prepared to kill every slaver on the ship. A place of hell was about to turn into a battleground.

Haunted by distressing memories, they couldn't help but notice the stark contrast between the dungeon and the rest of the slave ship. Overcoming the barrier that separated these two worlds was no easy feat. Yet, the dread of remaining in the dungeon paled in comparison to the terrifying unknown that awaited beyond its door.

There was no way out without being seen, except for Lilith. But Lilith couldn't leave the women alone. It was too risky for the women. They might as well be patient.

They hesitated with their sight on the entranceway and had no idea of their next move. The little time out of the shackles helped erase much of the awful feelings they had once held from being in bondage. At least they were still alive.

Eventually, the sudden rattle of keys startled the women. The lock on the door turned. But the women didn't move. They stood still with a sudden feeling of bravery.

"Listen!" said Lilith urgently. She nudged one of the ladies and pointed toward the shackle area. Lilith gave the woman a slight nod and kept her voice to a whisper.

This was it! The time had come. They paused for a moment and quickly found a place to hide. The door connecting the dungeon's staircase and the upper deck swung open. Then, everything changed.

Most women returned to their chained position and bent toward the deck. Four women hid beneath the stairs, two on each side of the railing. The guard was holding a wooden baton.

They watched bravely as the sailor shut the door and locked the bolts. Their eyes narrowed. Their breath quivered with tension as he moved slowly down the steps. While standing a few feet away, he paused for a moment as blood rushed through the women's veins and their heartbeats raced.

The women listened to every footstep coming down the staircase. It seemed like an eternity. They watched in silence.

The sailor turned his head toward the locked door and then turned his eyes toward the staircase. He paused momentarily, making an evil smile before continuing his walk forward. It was a privilege to be placed on guard duty for the women.

Slowly, he came closer, hitting the baton against the palm of his hand. They heard the keys rattling against his waist. The captives' hearts continued to pound as he slowly made his appointed round.

The sound of keys and the movement of footsteps ceased for a moment. Then his movement continued, and the keys rattled once again.

They waited on the sound of footsteps coming down the old staircase. They remained quiet, trying to map his every movement. Their pounding heartbeats and their wildest imaginations morphed into the mentality of vengeance.

There were, after all, weapons left behind by the dead sailors. Weaponry was distributed to the women on the side of the steps. They were well organized, blood rushing heavily through their veins and pounding hearts. They couldn't wait another minute!

When he came down the last set of steps, he was quickly snatched by the four women who dashed into motion, pulling him down the staircase and into the bloody dungeon. He was then met by fifty unchained women armed with anything they could confiscate as a weapon.

The sailor crawled around the ship's deck, trying to get his footing while grasping his baton. There was a gasp of awe as anger echoed in the deep shadow of the dungeon.

He managed to stand; despite the punishment he'd endured from the women. His emotion turned to confusion, his expression revealing his sudden shock. The same voices that had indulged him in pleasure now filled his soul with fear.

The sailor experienced a burst of strength and straightened his back, undeterred by the blood gushing down his face. He paused briefly, gazing around, yet the furious women offered no comfort as they stormed forward.

His face turned red, and his slippery feet wouldn't allow him to stand. The sailor lurched backward as his knees bent as he leaned forward, wobbling to the floor.

The woman quickly struck him in the head and began kicking him until there was no sign of movement. This was all part of their great struggle to survive and the beginning of much more.

Several hours had elapsed since the last guard ventured into the dungeon for routine inspection, and the other two were nowhere to be found. The crew aboard the ship couldn't help but ponder the fate of their fellow guards. The captain, too, was curious about the whereabouts of his top-ranking officers. He had always permitted his sailors to indulge themselves with the enslaved women, taking pleasure from their suffering. In the New World along the Mediterranean, this cruel act was regarded as heroic by his crew.

As reality dawned upon them, any enjoyment derived from the torment inflicted upon the enslaved women couldn't justify their absence from their posts. Should any of them reappear, mockery would ensue; however, no word came from the lost guards. Every ticking minute allowed for an opportunity for these women to devise a daring escape plan. Paralyzing fear consumed them as they reflected on endless nights of torment and dread, barely able to discern sounds and subtle movements.

Lilith took a deep breath, remembering the feeling of the shackles and abuse. The terrifying women promised to fight until death. Death was better than submission. Now the gloves were off, and the fight for freedom had begun.

The captain felt uneasy about the absent guards, interpreting their mute defiance as a mixture of fear and scornful culpability. As the tantalizing scent of freedom wafted around them, the women's hearts pounded with indignation.

Despite the passage of several hours, there was still no word from the guards. The crew's initial certainty gave way to bewilderment. Determined not to display any vulnerability, the captain refused to starve the women into submission. Instead, he dispatched a team of five sword-wielding sailors.

The women stared down at the corpses, whose eyes were wide open but whose bodies were stiff and dead. They dragged the dead guards into an empty room before their comrades entered the dungeon. They prepared for a full-blown war.

Lilith waited by the door's entrance, stashing her sword under the staircase before vanishing from her body.

When the sailors reached the dungeon, the women begged the guards not to slash them with their swords. They raised their hands in fear.

The sailors came closer with their swords drawn until they considered the threat had gone away. The missing sailors were no place to be found. The guards formed a defensive line. The women thought that they were going to die.

"There's no need to hurt us. We give up," one of the young ladies said. Lilith stayed quiet at the door's entrance, watching from a distance.

"Maybe you should tell us what happened," the guard shouted. "The missing lady did it while we watched in horror," she responded. "Then she escaped."

The sailors searched the dungeon while others chained the women. They found the headless bodies of the dead sailors, but Lilith remained unseen.

Lilith darted to the women with a bleak distaste for the sailor's ego. Still invisible, she stood there watching the sailors scold the women, but Lilith didn't allow this situation to end without a fight.

The sailor had grown silent with their eyes looking throughout the dungeon. She could not have escaped and simply vanished from the ship.

"Reckon, we will find her soon," one of the guards said, squeezing the young girl's jaw until she gave them more information. "I ask you again, where did she go?"

"She is right behind you, sir."

She smiled, knowing the sailor couldn't see Lilith and would never believe it. The guard still looked behind him, astonished, slowly turning his head away from the young girl.

The sailor heard a voice behind him saying, "My name is Lilith, the Angel of Vengeance." She was still invisible, so the sailor saw no one.

Lilith stepped back and grabbed the sword, cleaving the blade in the air before striking the sailor who had threatened the young girl. Lilith licked her lips as if she could taste the blood of her victims, already placing the thought of vengeance in her mind.

The scene was chilling - a group of terrified men stared as a sword mysteriously floated in mid-air, uncontrolled by any hand. Suddenly, Lilith struck the guard reaching for his own weapon. As the suspended sword hovered, a powerful voice demanded, "Free the girls!"

The guards couldn't see Lilith's face, but they could hear her feet stirring.

"Only one of you will survive to tell what you have seen," said the voice.

The guard's white faces stared at the sword hanging in mid-air. The tip of the blade touched one of the guards' necks. He could hardly breathe.

Their eyes were fixed on the sword's blade, and they struggled to breathe. A few moments passed without a sound, and their hopeless bodies seemed frozen in time. Their eyes looked around the room for the sound of the voice.

One of the soldiers started to run while tripping over the dead body of his comrade before the sword swiftly came after him.

"There is no point in running," the voice said while the other two guards begged for their lives. "Perhaps you shouldn't have come inside the dungeon. I'm a cast out angel from heaven. Go and tell your captain who I am. I will sink this ship and kill you if even a hair is harmed on these women."

The two guards dropped their weapons and ran, but Lilith threw the sword, piercing one in the back. In the blink of an eye, the guard fell dead as the other sailor ran hysterically up the staircase and out of the dungeon.

The women stood there, staring with their eyes focused on Lilith, who was still shivering from the action. Following Lilith's instructions, the ladies stayed in the dungeon, hoping the captain would free them once he heard the news.

The women were still trapped, hungry, and cold. Since being captured, the ladies never were allowed to breathe fresh air or feel the warmth of sunlight.

The freed sailor couldn't say anything. He stayed silent for a moment. He was in a strange shock and felt ashamed. There was no explanation. He looked like he'd seen a ghost. The terror in the dungeon nearly took his breath away. The sailors summoned the captain.

"How dare you run away, leaving your fellow soldiers in the dungeon without a fight?" asked the captain. "Where are the others?"

"They're all dead." The captain waited on the battle details, but the sailor was silent again. He was almost lifeless. The captain stared at him and didn't bother arguing the fact as if his lecturer was talking to a dead man.

"What have they done to you?" the captain asked.

"She is a spirit, and I couldn't see her body," said the sailor. "She isn't human. She's invisible. We never counted on her being a spirit. She's demonic."

The captain didn't believe a word. He glanced at the far end of the passageway that led to the stairs of the dungeon. "We will bury them there. They'll never see sunlight or eat from our gallery again."

The captain bore vengeance for the death of the sailors. Still, he was interested in exploring the Mediterranean and sought to gather as much resources as possible.

The captain placed two armed guards at the door and continued sailing. If true, what the freed sailor said didn't deter the captain. Maybe it was simply in his imagination the captain thought, but the night felt unpleasant as the air chilled with the extinguishment of twilight.

The sailor was confused, but his eyes were filled with tremendous fear. He was broken down by the strain of war and became paranoid. The fragile sailor began looking around, blinking his eyes and shaking uncontrollably.

His fellow sailors watched him shake himself back to reality. Then he leaped to his feet, screaming with energy. The other sailors stared at him momentarily, watching before slamming him back into his chair. He became motionless, holding his head toward the deck.

The captain ordered the freed sailor to be placed in confinement for the murder of the dead sailors. It was a whisper that the sailor had broken under stress. He had killed his comrades or left them in the hands of the captives to die. How could he do such an evil thing?

They wondered if what he told them might be true because no other person exited the dungeon alive.

The sailors stayed clear of the women in the dungeon. They didn't care about the surviving sailor's fate. He was nuts! The dungeon had turned into a curse. Some of the sailors became hostile and feared for their lives.

Suddenly, anger traveled throughout the ship, and there were glimpses of panic in the voices of the sailors. For the moment, they were safe. They busied themselves with chatter and gossip. The whole night the soldiers waited. Hour after hour, nothing happened apart from the waiting game.

Around midnight, while the guards drifted in and out of sleep, they heard a strange noise. A weird laughter from the dungeon followed by a gentle breeze that passed them. The guards murmured, breathing with constant fear. One of the guards lapsed into a swift silence.

The other guard said, "There is no need to panic." He lowered his head in a bit of bravery. The scene began to change. An eerie quiet fell over them.

Their faces, painted with fear, locked their eyes onto one another as they stood in the unnerving hallway. Suddenly, a sailor pounded on the door, commanding the ladies to keep quiet before attempting to peer through the narrow gap.

The soldier was blunt. "We're here to guard the door and don't want any trouble." He felt a chill going through his spine.

Only a bit of laughter descended from behind the walls of the bulkhead. There was a sudden coldness in the air. A blend of fresh air and a gust of wind came out of the dungeon.

Nothing was visible in the hallway, but the guards experienced a creepy, ghostly feeling. Maybe what the insane sailor said was true! Another chill and more laughter were coming from the dungeon.

The idea of a ghost ship or invisible woman gave way to exasperation as they stood guard at the dungeon's entrance. The guards glanced through the passageway of the ship.

Their hearts jumped at every noise that came out of the dungeon. Trying to imagine the women's plans, one of the braver guards whispered through the crevice of the door.

There came a gentle tap on the door of the dungeon. He leaned forward, resting his arms on the door.

"Are you alright in there?" he asked. His eyes shifted from side to side, feeling a bit of panic. He turned toward the door nervously before edging his way back to face the direction of the passageway. "I won't ask again," he said.

At first, the women refused to talk to him, but they finally conversed politely. Then, the soldiers reached out to converse and gather a little information on the women's motives. It was a common mistake, an error that Lilith wouldn't approve of at all.

The conversation led to simply a warning before the great rage began. "I'm sorry you were sent to secure this dungeon. We were brought here without our consent," said the voice behind the door. "Why won't you tell your captain to release us from this terrible place? Please give us something to eat and drink."

The guard's eyes snapped shut, and they both lapsed into silence. They heard the plea in her voice. They took a deep breath. One of the guards coughed. His face turned red, and his blue eyes glowed in the dark. He insisted he would talk to the captain. "But your captain ordered us to starve until death," said the voice.

Without warning, the doors rattled and clanged open with a burst of fire like lightning had struck an inferno. The mysterious flames surged with the intensity of a fast-moving tidal wave. The noise roared spreading out like a violent windstorm.

The pressure from the blast knocked both guards to the deck. They turned their faces and saw a tall shadow with two flaming swords approaching them. The tall shadow illuminated the hallway, and a mass of hot air followed from the dungeon.

The shadowy figure altered into a monster-like creature with multiple heads. It began to chase after the young soldiers. The image of the shadowy creature seemed to be flying in mid-air, moving swiftly toward the guards. They shouted in a fury of emotions.

The men made a forward dive and ran wildly down the passageway. Blood oozed down their faces and continued down their arms and legs. They ran down the aisle looking back at the creature with flaming blades coming after them.

The footsteps echoed, accompanied by a gust of wind. Suddenly, silence fell, and the chaotic noises ceased. The mysterious figure vanished into thin air, leaving them unharmed from their encounter with the towering, dark creature and the blazing orb of light. Although the towering, glowing shadow was gone, it had left behind a touch of mayhem.

The first guard ran into the room, screaming with his rank patched on his shoulders, indicating he was only a low-ranking seaman. Behind him came the other seaman, who ranked a little higher than the first, but still lower than most others on the ship. Both guards looked senseless, and they screamed ceaselessly. Their faces grew tight with their mouths wide opened. There was a tense silence before another series of high-pitched screams. His hands were wrapped around his body, and feeling for blood everywhere. He looked around at the soldiers with an accelerated heartbeat.

Their superior came running, trying to make sense of the sudden noise. He shouted their rank above the commotion but got no answer. "Stop screaming," said his superior.

The two guards seemed to be having a shouting contest. One of the sailors staggered, bowed his head in fear, and grabbed what he thought were wounds, but he was only drenched in sweat.

The other guard was in mild shock. He struggled to breathe and began clenching his hand to his chest. His body was trembling in fear, suffering from the aftershock and a racing heartbeat.

There was a sudden silence, except for the trembling in the guards breathing. The night was strange, and their fright caused a stir of emotions. They feared the tall flying shadow, but it was all in their heads.

Everyone was focused on the passageway that led to the dungeon. The sailors' eyes were glued to the dungeon with a death stare for a long moment. Nothing but silence! There was no way to get any sleep while the ship's crew was in disarray.

On the third day after the slaughter of the guards, a storm was brewing. When the ship shifted, the ship was sailing along the coast and there was a frosty chill. They'd been exploring the coastline looking for valuable treasure, agricultural commodities, livestock, or humans to enslave.

The confined women in the dungeon had not eaten in three to four days. The air was tense, and the captain had become like the Grim Reaper.

To the captain, the women were already dead. He waited for the women to become powerless. The cruelness of the fifth heavens had spoken and not a hint of respect for these enslaved victims.

There was a sudden surge in the ocean, shifting the energy of the waves. The captain looked fiercely at the falling sky, bringing an intense storm.

Billowing clouds expanded across the sky, casting an eerie darkness as a looming storm brewed. Whipping winds and relentless rain filled the air, creating an unsettling atmosphere. Lilith remained a fugitive, escaping the grasp of the fifth heaven's deities who saw her betrayal to the outer realm as unforgivable treason.

The sickness, torture, and continued weeping from the women were compounded by the treachery of blind hatred. There was no peace in the dungeon. Their minds were seized by anger and a great fear of the surging tides.

There was so much tension; it was a kind of vengeance that only death could solve. A need for reprisal crept into their inner thoughts.

The sealed dungeon became a dark place without sleep while robbing the women of their freedom. It was like the women were frozen in time, and the captain was determined to forget all about them until he was sure death had found them.

The women lived trapped inside the bloody dungeon, where they spent their days and nights with no food, water, or the smell of fresh air.

Though her sight was hazy, Lilith thirsted for revenge. She declared, "Life has its moments - times to weep, to heal, to love, and to find harmony. But there are also moments to wage war." She paused momentarily before continuing, "Our battle reaches beyond mere mortals; it pits us against sinister authorities. We must confront the wicked entities dominating parts of the celestial realm. Ultimately, there are adversaries even more powerful than these sailors we must face."

The vessel shook, yet Lilith inspired the women to display courage and persist in their battle against the sinister force stealing their souls through trickery, deceit, and murder. This cruel force greedily robbed the world of harmony for its own twisted satisfaction. These malicious deities from the outer realm arrived like stealthy burglars under the cover of darkness. The wind unleashed a ghastly howl, and the Mediterranean's waves crashed into the ship, sweeping a sailor overboard.

There was a momentary silence before a lightning bolt struck the ship's hull. The bolt malevolently targeted the vessel's foundation. Chaos and terror erupted within the dungeon as lightning bolts filled the imprisoned women with fear. The waterway radiated an ominous aura as the women remained confined below deck. That fateful night, their destiny lay in Lilith's hands.

The women were yelling out as Lilith stood quietly, eyes locked on the dungeon's door. The arcs of light came piercing through the darkened sky into the dungeon's prison. The turbulence came from every direction.

The dungeon was under siege! A distraught lady stood nearby, shedding tears as her heart weighed heavy with distress. Her cheeks were drenched in a stream of sorrow, and fear of the impending doom painted her face. Her sorrowful wounds ran deeper than words could describe.

There was no mistaking the tears. What they needed was a miraculous deliverance. They stemmed from deep sorrow and a desire for freedom. The women felt the waves rocking the ship from side to side and the pulsating wind suddenly coming out of thin air.

Most importantly, the fifth heavens were not the sole otherworldly force. The formidable seventh heavens remained, with the all-powerful Creator vigilantly overseeing every aspect of creation.

Out on the ocean, something akin to a fiery orb gleamed on the distant horizon. Its radiant light mirrored the sun's brilliance as it approached the vessel, trailed by a thunderous roar.

The immense fireball weaved an electric arc before soaring gracefully onto the blue sea. Engulfing the fifth heavens' ominous clouds, the fireball continued its luminous journey.

Vibrant lightning bolts painted the night sky with shades of reddish-brown, green, purple, and white, casting a mesmerizing glow. The women, moved by the spectacle, shed tears of joy as intense bursts of lightning preceded a surreal calm.

Meanwhile, sailors on deck scrambled in panic. As the monumental clash unfolded, divine intervention from the seventh heavens shielded the women. Safeguarded by celestial forces, they lived through their ordeal in the dreadful dungeon's depths.

The dungeon transformed into a sanctuary of protection amidst the looming terror. Nothing delightful lingered within the pitch-black void. Their hearts quivered, feeling the ship shudder as the waves' crests collided against it. Possibly, the mysterious events unfolding outside the dungeon served as a miraculous blessing for these women.

The waves crashed onto the ship's deck, sweeping some sailors into the ocean's grasp. Among them was the frantic sailor guarding the dungeon door, suddenly consumed by the sea's depths.

The wind struck the ship in the moment of justice, turning the tides in favor of the helpless women in the dungeon. The women were fine. They all realized that they had survived the terrible ordeal of the plague of hatred targeted against them.

After a fierce battle, the sinister forces of the cosmos were defeated, leaving the sailors to fend for themselves. They had no strength without the fifth heavens.

The sailors were locked in darkness and confused before sinking to the bottom of the sea. Some stumbled down the dungeon passageway, trying to find refuge from the inferno and arcs of lightning. There was screaming and trembling magnified by echoes from the dying lips of the slavers. Fear surged, causing a wave of emotions amid the turmoil.

The lightning flashed enough force to shake the ship into a sudden panic. The terrifying storm brought a wild rage of commotion throughout the ship.

The wind was like a weapon, and the illuminated fire carried the kiss of death. The captain drifted out of his safe haven into Lilith's arms. In a moment, he was taken into the dungeon. The feeling of revenge was way too strong for Lilith to feel pity for the man. His submission was only a recipe for death.

He stumbled in darkness in a daze of ignorance, but the women remained heartless in the dungeon. His tears flowed like a fountain in this moment of terror. The light of justice had condemned him to the grave of the ship's dungeon.

The agony of his terror was stripped away as though he were being controlled by a powerless, wicked spirit. He was helpless. His spirit was too weak, and his physical body was sweaty. He was limp with fatigue, and twinges of pain haunted the sockets of his joints.

A blast caused blood to roll down his head, and he stumbled like a drunken stupor. His body twisted with fear with each frustrated movement. His voice was steady with emotion, but he had a fearful appearance. His mask of bravery faded away in the darkness as if his thoughts and dreams had been captured by an angel of death.

He thrust his arms in the air and fell to his knees to acknowledge his loss of superior status. He was quickly lifted back up to his feet by the women. His pathetic voice became more of a frustrated groan as his boldness disappeared.

The way Lilith was feeling, she was handed the position to sit in judgment of the slavers. And she did it joyfully!

Every remaining sailor had to defend himself, and confusion spread rapidly throughout the ship. The elegance of the seventh heavens had shattered the captain's glorious past.

The captain was confined, his hands and feet tied and shackled in iron. His body was fastened in place as he lay sprawled in an old iron chair like a common criminal. His eyes were running with tears, and there was no more source of power. The fifth heavens had made empty promises, and his life ended in disgrace.

At the end of the evening, the danger had dissipated. The high spirit of the enemy began to fade away. The rest of the women suddenly rushed out of the dungeon and fought wildly against their former oppressors.

They overcame their impulse of fear, and the scale of justice was reversed. They had prayed to the Creator for deliverance from the chains. The captain's strength was gone as he watched the women preparing for battle. The ship's depth brought terror, and his ego was destroyed at the sight of his dead sailors' bodies piled up in the dungeon.

Lilith became the villain and the staunch enemy of the fifth heavens. She was once loyal to the fifth heavens, but now she had changed allegiance to a righteous cause.

The Creator had rescued her from the clutches of hate's scourge. The wicked beings who pledged loyalty to the fifth celestial realm had lost their grip. Their influence over the women had abruptly dissipated.

The women's journey began where the drainage divides, sailing toward the Nile-Congo Watershed deeper into Central Africa. There was no more supremacy and a place to live their life without fear. Perhaps, the gods of the fifth heaven would be hard to penetrate the mysterious life of the Congo as if their powers were limited and harder to influence with empty promises.

It was once thought impossible that pagan gods could ever infiltrate the pure, enchanting realm of the Congo. This idea may have held some weight, had these deities not manifested their fury with a glittering wave of riches. However, the deities cunningly employed materialism and the illusion of unmatched power to cast a dark veil over their beneficiaries.

For ages, Congo had remained unscathed by foreign gods, transforming into a refuge for women and anyone else fortunate enough to reach its coasts. Still, the ominous unrest of distant realms loomed ominously, closely observing the Central African nation for the perfect opportunity to strike. With their arrival in Congo, Lilith and her female companions were met with open arms by the local people.

Amid the power struggle between the pagan gods of the fifth heavens and the seventh heavens, the situation became broader and more intricate. The seventh heavens agreed to be the protector of Congo only if the Congolese served the Creator with reverence. It was impossible to venerate the fifth heavens in any way and win the heart of the Creator God.

Still, the women lived on the edge, knowing that the pagan gods existed and the fifth heavens were waiting for Congo to become their prey. But what Lilith wanted more than anything was to live without fear.

She knew very well what the fifth heavens were capable of doing. There weren't any remaining thoughts of the past battles but whatever the future might endure. They had to maintain good daily habits nurturing the words of the Creator with reverence.

CHAPTER 8

IN THE NEW KINGDOM, foreigners came to experience the elegance of Egypt as each new province was incorporated into the empire. Instead of using war for his goals, the young Amenhotep IV favored peaceful solutions, employing more cunning strategies than the pharaohs before him.

He changed his name to Akhenaten and established a new monotheistic religion that believed the sun's power was life-giving and life-sustaining. Akhenaten built a new place of worship dedicated to the sun god, Aten.

He prayed to Aten daily, ordering the priests to tear down all statues and images of Egypt's polytheistic gods. He exalted Aten:

"You arise beauteous in the horizon of the heavens, Oh living
Aten who creates life.
When you shine forth in the Eastern horizon, You fill every
land with your beauty.
You are so beautiful and great, Gleaming and high over
every land.
Your rays embrace the lands and all you have created; You
are Re and reach out to all your creations,
And hold them for your beloved Son.
You are afar, but your rays touch the Earth; Men see you
but know not your ways."

The elevated statue of Amun, the holiest of all gods in Egypt, was cast down, becoming a vanishing shadow in the dust of dawn.

"You rise in perfection on the horizon of the sky, living Aten, who started life. When you rise upon the eastern horizon, you fill every land with perfection."

Akhenaten passionately praised Aten while accusing Amun's priests of stealing. He labeled Thebes as a city teeming with sensual gods but declared that Aten's radiant light would banish them into eternal darkness.

> "When you rise from the horizon, the Earth grows bright;
> You shine as the Aten in the sky and drive away the darkness;
> When your rays gleam forth, the whole of Egypt is festive.
> People wake and stand on their feet, For you have lifted them.
> They wash their limbs, take up their clothes, and dress;
> They raise their arms to you in adoration."

The citizens of the Egyptian Empire and the Israelites living in Egypt were strongly influenced by Hellenistic culture. Every prayer in the Egyptian or Israelite territory ended with the pagan god Amen, or Amun-Ra of Thebes.

The worship of Amen expanded across Mesopotamia, reaching Ethiopia, Nubia, Libya, Syria, and even Palestine. As time went by, Christianity embraced the term Amen within its daily prayers.

Akhenaten's great-grandfather, Thutmose III, stormed across the Middle East and the gold-laden lands of Nubia. Egyptians set up a formidable military presence beyond Syria's boundaries. This triumphant conquest secured Egypt's position as the richest and most dominant nation in the world.

In every newly conquered province, the defeated people were governed by a high priest or vizier, appointed by the pharaoh. This vizier acted as a religious leader and oversaw tax collection and tribute payments, which contributed to Egypt's expansion into an empire. The Israelites, meanwhile, enjoyed a privileged status under Thutmose III and led a luxurious life in Egyptian territories. Their prosperity and special treatment were considered miraculous.

Both the Israelites and native Egyptians had once been enslaved, but together, they managed to break free from their oppressors – the Hyksos. These Balkan settlers from a lower social class sought power, treasure, agricultural riches, and opportunities to elevate their families into the upper class.

The Egyptians adopted new military strategies from the Hyksos, such as deploying powerful horse-drawn chariots that allowed them to dominate significant parts of the Mediterranean region.

The Hyksos swept in and took over the Nile Delta, making a mark in Palestine as powerful rulers before setting up their capital at Avaris in Lower Egypt. This forced surrounding territories, such as Palestine, Israel, Nubia, and the Nile Delta heartlands to show their loyalty through tribute payments. Egyptian culture and the Israelites' relationship within Egypt were transformed significantly by the Hyksos.

A cosmic energy took over the religious landscape of Egypt, giving rise to a strong sect dedicated to the sun god who safeguarded the nation. Though the Hyksos were formidable adversaries, elements of their religion were entwined with Egypt's ruling system. It became synonymous with wealth, playing a major role in shaping both politics and religious dynamics within Egypt.

In a deep glow of darkness, the scene changed that crippled the religious culture of the Nile. The Hyksos gods merged into daily life when the Indo-Aryans invaded the Nile Delta and began living on Egyptian soil.

The Egyptians and Israelites were inseparable throughout the Old Kingdom and the beginning of the New Kingdom. They had endured pain and were enslaved together by the Hyksos settlers. The pharaoh gave the Israelites special status and granted them tax exemptions, along with the most fertile land along the eastern delta of the Nile.

The agricultural and pastoral lifestyle of the Israelites helped save Egypt from a severe famine during the time of Thutmose III.

The pharaohs extended their gratitude to future generations. When it came to war, the Israelites gave their best soldiers to serve in the Egyptian military. The Israelites eventually prospered and multiplied to the degree that made ordinary citizens bitter.

The human mind is very selective and often forgets things it chooses to ignore. The Egyptians didn't take long to forget the miraculous benefits of Israelites living on Egyptian soil.

The Egyptians were blinded by bigotry injected into the fabric of the empire by the Hyksos. In Egypt, the standard for success involved trusting polytheistic gods in their daily lives.

Wealth flowed into Egypt from the fertile Nile Valley—from the limestone hills through the sandy desert into Thebes. In the eastern desert lay the Nile and the Red Sea, which supported a nomadic population and contained massive mineral deposits.

To the northeast, trade routes between the Isthmuses of the Suez and the Mediterranean Sea brought much-needed timber, copper, and excellent trade relations with the Lebanese port city.

Thutmose III welcomed captured children into Egypt, giving them a chance to live as proud citizens rather than slaves or war enemies. By lifting their spirits, he made them feel that Egypt was even more glorious than their homeland.

The children were then returned to their native land to help rule the pharaoh's defeated foes. At the center of Thutmose III's rule was the chief god Amun of Thebes, the sun god Ra, and other minor, earthly gods which the Israelites found attractive.

The viziers, who were esteemed officials primarily selected from the royal family for their allegiance to the pharaoh, played an essential role. They were appointed to govern as overseers of the "gold countries," ensuring a continuous inflow of gold and other resources into the Egyptian economy.

Egypt ascended to global prominence as innovative ideas and abundant resources fueled its flourishing economy, solidifying its position as the world's leading superpower. Shrewd viziers and elites skillfully managed the inflow of wealth, ensuring it reached every corner of their vibrant marketplace. Simultaneously, the priests played an essential role in bridging the gap between the people and the mystical realm, upholding harmony and interpreting the gods' daily messages.

The priests were the peacekeepers between the gods and ordinary people. They also performed religious and political duties.

Like the Greeks, the Egyptians came to believe gods lived in statues and resided in temples. Only the priests or priestesses were allowed to enter the sacred enclosure in the presence of the god statue.

The power of the Egyptians and Israelites was an enigma. They combined Greek and Hyksos fighting techniques, creating a dominant force in the Nile Delta. Courageous on the battlefield, the Israelites supported Egypt in overcoming adversaries. The spoils of war brought annual tributes from conquered villages seeking Egypt's protection, and provided soldiers with a reliable income.

Prince Moses, Commander of the Southern Cavalry, led a raid into Hermopolis and helped take the city back from the Ethiopians. During the battle, the Israelites saved the Egyptians from a humiliating defeat.

Prince Moses was an Israelite by blood but was raised as an Egyptian. There were rumors of the prince being an Israelite at a time when the Israelites were rejected as privileged citizens.

During Akhenaten's reign, the royal family maintained its power by marrying close relatives. The princes and princesses held exceptional influence and enriched the royal family with their artistic talents.

Nefertiti, whose name means "a beautiful woman has come," was the queen of Egypt and Akhenaten's wife. She supported her husband with innovative ideas and played a significant role in advancing the new sun cult of Aten.

It is believed that Nefertiti was of royal lineage—a princess from Mitanni in northern Mesopotamia. Some speculate that her family descended from the Minoans of Crete, a civilization that ruled the Aegean Island and had strong cultural connections to Egypt.

Her features were indeed foreign to Egypt, and a woman of mysterious appeal and beauty captivated the court with features that not even the young prince could ignore.

Egypt was a true superpower in the Mediterranean, but the Hittites had a clear advantage because their ports lay at the mouth of Lebanon. The Hittites were as brave and daunting on the battlefield as the Egyptians.

Nefertiti brought a more binding pact with Mitanni and sealed the alliance that increased the Egyptian's sea power against the Hittites.

Even after the Hyksos invasion, the Minoans remained master shipbuilders and their artistic culture revolutionized Mitanni through lavish decorations and architecture. This transformation spread Minoan-style artwork across the Mediterranean region.

Nefertiti represented the female aspect within the divine triad comprised of Pharaoh Akhenaten, his queen, and Aten. The relationship between the gods and humanity mirrored that of kings and their subjects.

The young prince and future king of the Egyptian Empire transformed the nation with revolutionary ideas.

Akhenaten's family had ruled Egypt for nearly two hundred years before he changed his name from Amenhotep IV, meaning, "Amun is Pleased." The king built a new holy city called Amarna, bringing new customs and religious ideas to Egypt.

In Akhenaten's first year as ruler, the world experienced one of the most devastating events in history – the Minoan eruption of Thera.

This catastrophic volcanic explosion not only annihilated Thera Island, but also caused severe damage to nearby Minoan settlements and agricultural lands along the Cretan coast. The disaster didn't stop there, as earthquakes and tsunamis followed, affecting regions as far as Egypt. Crete and Egypt, once close trading allies, found their relationship strained when numerous Cretans sought refuge in the Egyptian Empire.

A terrible rumble instigated by the fifth heavens filled the air with banging thunder echoes from the darkened sky. The foreign gods brought brutality and desperation to the nation through vengeance. The wind roared with an awful fury.

The foreign gods lured the covenant nation away from their greatest source of blessings simply by replacing the Omnipotent Creator. These new pagan gods of the Egyptian domain turned the nation into a weak empire.

The Egyptians enthusiastically embraced the new deities, while the Israelites gradually adapted to this fascinating tradition, leading to a decreased devotion to Yahweh.

Sekhmet, the goddess of destruction, was portrayed holding the ankh and entered Crete on a vengeful warpath. Sekhmet, meaning "the powerful one," was known as both the "lady of terror" and the "lady of life" due to her dual role in creation and destruction.

In an attempt to pacify the mighty goddess, the Egyptians reverently constructed statues, exalting her as a paramount deity. According to Egyptian mythology, Sekhmet served as the Eye of Ra and was dispatched to bring down those who turned against Ra.

Eventually, the Egyptians acknowledged Ra as the architect of the cosmos, and his influence spread throughout the nation. In appreciation of the sun's life-giving properties and their belief in his bestowal of life, they crafted statues in Ra's image, honoring him as their primary deity.

Even the high priest became afraid when the ash clouds from the volcanic eruption blocked the sun's glowing rays. The shadow from the ash gave the sun a strange appearance.

The Eye of Ra darkened the sky as volcanic ash interrupted the natural order of the seasons in the Mediterranean.

Occasionally, the Ankh was passed on to the pharaohs, indicating both the gift of life and the purifying power of water. The Ankh symbolized life and was associated with the journey into the eternal afterlife.

The promise of everlasting life through resurrection was extended to the royal family through hieroglyphics and iconographic art, invoking the gods' protection.

The primary objective of the enigmatic fifth heavens was to captivate the minds of the Egyptians, spreading its mystical pagan influence across the Mediterranean and along the Nile, consolidating its inherent powers. The Hyksos, lacking sufficient physical force to conquer Crete or Africa, focused on erasing their subjects' spiritual awareness and substituting it with captivating myths that maintained control.

These pagan myths functioned like a mystical road map. The polytheistic gods blossomed in areas of the Mediterranean and along the Nile, changing the shape of spirituality.

The fascinating mythologies of the fifth heavens spread their mystique all along the Nile Valley, reaching from the embrace of the Aegean Sea to the furthest corners of Ethiopia, Egypt, and Nubia. In a twist of fate, the enigmatic realm of these fifth heavens bestowed upon Sudan a tragic and deadly curse.

Two years after becoming king, Akhenaten built this new city in honor of Aten and moved the capital from Thebes.

Upon ascending the throne, Akhenaten implemented revolutionary changes in Egypt, promoting artistic and religious movements that recognized Aten, the sun disc, as the supreme god. Aten's radiant disc was often depicted with small ankhs at the ends of its rays, symbolizing immortality and the bread of life.

The pharaoh banished all previous deities, including Amun-Ra, who was highly revered by the priestly class. Atenism shifted faith from polytheism to monotheism, acknowledging the belief in a single god. However, it retained the most famous and widespread symbol - the ankh, also known as the cross of life.

The hieroglyphic symbol of sandal straps embodied the beauty of life. Sandals were an essential part of daily life in Egypt, and Osiris was often depicted rising from his coffin, clasping an ankh in each hand.

In the captivating belief system of Atenism, traditional idols became obsolete. Aten, the divine sun disc, enthralled worshippers with its majestic rays of light, presenting a distinct form of devotion. This rejuvenating spiritual practice in Egypt demanded exclusive allegiance to Aten or Akhenaten, forsaking all other gods.

In ancient Egypt, Akhenaten and his queen, Nefertiti, were the sole connection to Aten, the country's one true deity. Followers of their new faith could wear the ankh—the emblem of Aten—symbolizing physical life and the human soul's journey in the afterlife. The rise of Atenism stirred up multiple reactions; some switched loyalties out of fear, while others did so out of ambition and desire for power. Akhenaten implemented a stringent code, with only a handful of men daring to remain neutral.

Disobedience led to harsh demands and brutal consequences, as one had to declare loyalty to Aten just to be part of the royal inner circle. Everyone was forced to conceal any loyalty they had for other gods.

The monotheistic god, Aten, was on the move to revolutionize and control all religious affairs. Some had sold out their fellow citizens for profit and shared nothing in common with Atenism. It was a rough transition, but some benefited from the massive labor assignments and government services paying for most relocation expenses.

Prince Moses was a firm believer in a single, all-powerful God, yet he constantly battled against the spiritual obscurity brought on by Atenism. Aten's philosophy revolved around the sun's disc-giving and life-sustaining abilities. Amun-Ra, the sun god, shared an affinity with Aten – both symbolizing the sun.

During Akhenaten's reign, Egypt evolved into a peaceful and idealistic nation for its citizens. The abandonment of warfare marked a significant shift, as Egypt had not previously considered war obsolete until this pharaoh instituted such changes.

Amenhotep IV changed his name to Akhenaten, while Nefertiti adopted the name Neferneferuaten-Nefertiti, which means "the Aten is radiant of radiance for the beautiful one has come," to honor the newfound reverence for the god Aten, the sun disc.

Akhenaten moved his capital from Thebes to a new location called Tell el Amarna on the east side of the Nile River. The new city was built on the desert bay, which the pharaoh called Akhetaten, showing monotheism of sun worship.

Nestled along the Nile's west bank, Necropolis in Amarna was a thriving city of the dead. It housed royal tombs and sacred shrines, with laborers and craftsmen attending to the needs of the royal family. This flourishing city became Egypt's crowning jewel, boasting the Royal Wadi—a channel constructed amidst towering cliffs that redirected Nile waters away from burial chambers while still permitting sunshine to grace tomb entrances.

Merchants, temples, consuls, viziers, and magnificent structures filled this vibrant city. Akhetaten (Amarna), the new royal city, was brimming with life as it sat proudly within the Amarna Desert between two majestic mountains—its creation a tribute to Atenism.

The image of Akhenaten dominated the city, along with portrayals of Nefertiti and her daughters engaged in ceremonial activities. The pharaoh altered all religious practices by initiating Aten as the sole god of Egypt and ordered the Imperial Army to work on the construction of a new sacred city.

Akhenaten made no apology—he even threatened his general, who attempted to halt construction by using the soldiers as laborers. The soldiers were forced to build the new splendid city of Amarna.

Akhenaten went against his general and civil authorities by abandoning Thebes and neglecting his mighty army.

The pharaoh's resolve grew stronger in his pursuit of a distinct, architecturally innovative capital city situated between the cliffs and dedicated to Aten. The Egyptian and Israelite cultures bore great resemblance in their belief systems and languages before the Hyksos incursion, sharing similar Hebrew dialects, and worshiping the one true God, Yahweh.

Designated as the chosen people from the Hebrew race, the Israelites enjoyed a privileged status in Egypt due to their unwavering devotion to Yahweh, who wasn't represented through an idol. In gratitude for their allegiance and compliance, the Israelites received divine blessings of love, peace, and prosperity as part of a covenant with God.

However, this divine love became trapped in time – resentment and avarice led to the rejection of Thutmose III's special status. Consequently, the unique standing of the Israelites was seized abruptly, like a thief in the night.

Over time, the Israelites thrived and multiplied in number. However, they inadvertently began embracing new gods introduced by settlers from the Balkans. Once renowned for their monotheistic beliefs and high moral standards in Egypt, the Israelites gradually succumbed to the allure of idolatry.

Thutmose III, an undefeated national hero, was highly esteemed in Egypt and secured a pledge of loyalty from the Israelites. However, as fear and jealousy crept into the hearts of ordinary citizens, it sparked a shift in their relationship with the Israelites. The Israelite community grew remarkably, outshining any special treatment they received from Egyptian authorities as they thrived in everyday life.

Egypt was rich in domestic animals, ample hunting opportunities, and an array of birds flourishing in its marshlands. The land yielded a variety of vegetables and fruit-heavy vineyards featuring figs, berries, grapes, and pomegranates, alongside abundant wheat and barley for bread-making. The Israelites' presence brought incredible gifts and the wonders of miraculous blessings to Egypt.

Nestled between the Nile Valley and the western Sahara Desert, precious rock salt was collected from the sea's crusted shoreline. The Egyptians no longer relied on the Israelites for sustenance, as Joseph's oath faded from memory. Fueled by whispers of envy, the Israelites lost their sanctuary and witnessed their earthly paradise transform into a harsh nightmare.

The gradual denial of promises led to the Israelites losing their esteemed status in society. Caught off guard as the power structure snatched away all they held dear; the Israelites faced a tragic end to their peaceful and prosperous lives in Egypt. Once cherished, they now found themselves as outcasts and second-class citizens in a land they had loved for generations.

The Egyptians initially targeted the Israelites by seizing their grazing lands and fertile fields. The most significant change in their relationship was the eventual enslavement within the Egyptian Empire. This bondage involved the subjugation of dark-skinned individuals by other black and brown people. Egyptians held a strong belief in their own superiority, considering themselves above all other humans - even the European settlers who introduced the caste system and polytheism to Egypt.

The viziers and elders of Egypt came to the Pharaoh saying, "Behold, the people of the children of Israel are greater and mightier than we. Therefore, counsel us on what to do with them until we gradually destroy them from among us."

Torn by his love for the Israelites, the Pharaoh hesitated. Yet, yearning to maintain his people's respect, he ultimately succumbed to the pressure. "Every male boy born to the Israelites must be thrown into the Nile."

The Egyptians adopted a new kind of brutality, driven by a desire for cultural superiority. Physical aggression became increasingly prevalent and met little resistance from the Israelites. The situation bore a striking resemblance to life under the oppressive Hyksos regime. While ruling Egypt, the Hyksos subjected both Egyptians and Israelites to slavery and harsh physical punishments, causing blood to spill in the name of discipline. These two groups found themselves at the lowest tier of the Eurocentric caste system's pyramid.

The alliance with Joseph concluded, emphasizing the significance of astrology and showcasing the celestial entities from the fifth heavens. The Israelites' unique status was supplanted by compulsory labor. They constructed magnificent royal palaces, underground tombs, and intricate burial sites for the deceased.

CHAPTER 9

The angel Raphael was still in the midst of a nightmare, trying to convince the Egyptians and the Israelites to abide by the covenant of brotherhood. Over time, he discovered that achieving a crucial victory wouldn't be a walk in the park; instead, it would be an intense, prolonged battle against the enigmatic pagan gods of the outer world.

He wanted to see the black and brown people unite against the spiritual forces of darkness and trust in the Creator God for their protection. There would be no protection for the Egyptians or Israelites as long as they hung on to these pagan gods and neglected the Creator God. It was exhausting for him to share his wisdom because he continued living a servitude life. Raphael was still an outcast and an alien to Egypt because he wasn't born of Egyptian blood.

While the moonlight scattered various shades of light over Thebes, Raphael was caught in a dream in which a team of angels from the seventh heavens tested his strength. A sudden gush of wind came over the sandy hills out of the deep blue sky.

In a restless daze, Raphael saw a gigantic star hovering in the heavens. Inside the huge star was a great mountain burning with fire. The mountain burned day and night. The inferno was horrible, and a fearful sight.

One of the angels said to him, "This place is the prison for the cast out angels who afflicted, oppressed, destroyed, made war, and caused trouble on the Earth, and here they will be imprisoned forever."

The angels took Raphael to a river of fire, which flowed like water into a great lake, and then to a peak that reached the heavens. From there, they went to another location and saw seven magnificent mountains, all taking different forms. There were precious stones and treasures in the uttermost depths of the Earth.

Amid the mountains were beautiful trees with a wonderful fragrance beyond imagination and leaves that bloomed during all seasons. He saw another landscape high in the mountains with groves of trees that produced flowing nectar.

Beyond the mountains were aloe trees, almond trees, and a variety of fruit trees with sweet aromas.

As he looked north, high above the mountain, he saw fragrant trees of cinnamon and pepper. There were also two magnificent trees with forbidden fruits, magnificent in height.

The Tree of Knowledge had glorious leaves with holy fruits that, if eaten, would bestow great wisdom.

Raphael exclaimed, "How beautiful is the tree, and how attractive is it look!"

The vizier touched Raphael above the shoulders, and his dream ceased. Raphael's face appeared frightened from the vision.

"Why are you sleeping here?" the vizier asked while turning in the direction of the palace.

Raphael sensed the vizier didn't acknowledge his confused mind or his vision from heaven. They walked toward the palace, the vizier in the lead.

Inside the palace, people danced to a joyous celebration, with the priests offering silent prayers to Amun of Thebes.

A sound echoed between the walls. It was a voice deep with sarcasm. Akhenaten was planning to abandon Thebes. The situation was bizarre and catastrophic for the priests of Amun.

There was a high-pitched cry as the portrait of the beautiful queen Nefertiti from Mitanni was about to be removed from the royal palace.

The priests came down the hallway carrying torches, illuminating the temple's north side.

The radiant beam of light glared off the famous bust of Nefertiti. Her long dark hair was crafted firmly beneath her bust. It was designed by Amenhotep III's favorite sculptor, Djhutmose, the official court sculptor of the pharaoh.

Nefertiti's bust was a fascinating artwork carved from limestone and gypsum plaster with shades of red, green, blue, and glittering gold.

The bust was the symbol of royal perfection and served as an iconic blue crown of feminine beauty. The creative artwork dazzled in all its beauty as singing and dancing entertained the royal family and their guests in the splendid Malkata Palace.

The palace walls were decorated with heroic figures and artwork supporting their political and religious beliefs. The famous flaming hieroglyphic ankh with the eye of Ra was perfectly carved into the wall. The ceiling was decorated with brilliant golden and blue to imitate the sky with the astronomical likeness of the outer world.

Nefertiti sang with a captivating voice, filling the room with her impeccable tone. The queen's lyrics were simply magnificent. Her enchanting voice and elegant demeanor held the audience spellbound.

As she danced, the young pharaoh Akhenaten couldn't help but rise to his feet, vividly recalling his first glimpse of Nefertiti and the lust her beauty ignited within him. The palace attendants appeared entranced, seemingly bewitched by her endless energy. Her voice was comparable—and sometimes superior—to the illustrious singers who performed for the royal throne.

Her melodious voice resonated like heavenly tunes, drawing both guests and semi-nude performers to its center. Nefertiti held the audience captive with the radiant energy of her performance. It was truly a brilliant spectacle!

Raphael returned carrying the most exquisite food and drinks. The banquet hall was filled with flaming torches along the palace's walls.

The important thing now was to keep the royal family and guests happy, and nothing else mattered.

There was nothing Nefertiti loved more than dancing and entertaining her guests. Her laughter and flirting brightened the room with her charming smile. Her father's mood stiffened again, turning his head toward the noisy crowd.

His mind seemed to echo with unpleasant thoughts, but Nefertiti loved every moment of her dancing. She twisted and turned among the guests.

Everyone was watching the queen's performance with a certain glow. She was very beautiful, and her attire captured the splendor and wealth of royalty.

In front of her sat the newly crowned pharaoh in his beautifully carved chair made of the finest gold. The mosaic patterns on the marble floor seemed to glow when touched by any rays of light. The King leaned forward while sitting in the chair with his arm crossed, his eyes glued on the queen.

The king had a thin frame and an elongated head and arms. His awkward appearance brought mockery whenever he was on the dance floor. The audience teased and joked as his arms flared with the wobbliness of his movements.

Someone shouted at Raphael above the crowd's roar, "Stop standing around!"

Raphael found himself pushed aside, his breath hitching as memories of being chained up overwhelmed him. A voice called out his name, jolting him back to reality and reminding him that he now served in the royal palace.

Overwhelmed with nerves, Raphael's thoughts strayed from the happenings in the ballroom. He was preoccupied with his recent separation from the seventh heavens and his love for Lilith. He hadn't seen her since leaving the ship and desperately hoped she was safe. Shaking his head to refocus, Raphael continued on his path, unable to ignore the growing tension in the palace and the praises of Amun-Ra.

Queen Mother Tiye, beaming as she greeted her Nubian guests, briefly experienced frustration upon noticing her servants. The room, momentarily enveloped in a somber silence, soon regained its lively atmosphere. Thanks to Tiye's firm stance on political and religious matters, she confidently navigated foreign affairs and wielded considerable influence over the Pharaoh.

Endowed with innate wisdom, Queen Mother Tiye and her guests shifted from discussing politics to reveling in delightful camaraderie at the grand banquet. As guests arrived, they were met with steaming cups of tea and sumptuous dishes on gleaming silver trays. Laughter and cheer enveloped the room, accompanied by dancing, singing, and captivating performances—a precious moment of respite from the weight of political matters.

Everyone seemed unaware of the inner thoughts of the pharaoh, as though some intricate force had directed their minds. It was strange, but abandoning Thebes wasn't part of the topic. Whatever the reason, the celebration brought everyone together. The negative voices were all gone.

Afterward, happiness turned from a delicate festivity to deep divisiveness between the priesthood and royalty.

A tense conflict was simmering between the priests and the royal family's supporters, who aimed to eliminate Egypt's polytheistic deities—particularly Amun, a beloved figure among the masses. The cult of Amun had become deeply entrenched in every facet of Egyptian life. Amun-Ra bestowed credibility upon many in the upper class, elevating the priestly caste to a status nearly on par with the pharaoh.

Even commoners attributed Egypt's prosperity to Amun. A significant shift occurred as efforts to defund the cult of Amun increased, redirecting funds towards the monotheistic faction that revered Aten – the radiance of the sun's rays.

As Akhenaten ascended to the throne and Nefertiti became the distinguished Great Royal Wife, Aten was merely an unremarkable deity among other minor gods. Egyptian priests were soon commanded to shift their loyalty to Aten, previously an insignificant god, and prepare for a move from Thebes to a brand-new royal capital, Amarna.

By the fifth year of Akhenaten's reign, Aten ascended as the supreme deity in Egyptian worship. Rumors circulated that the era of Amun had ended, and the temple's treasures must either be willingly surrendered or forcibly seized by the royal palace. The world surrounding the priests grew perilous, and the nation became a frightening place for those who refused to embrace Atenism.

Akhenaten stated, "The High Priest of Amun had been judged by Aten, who watches over Egypt now." All things were at the protection of the new faith in Aten that threatened the powerful elites.

The rituals performed by the priesthood were replaced by daily prayers performed by the royal family, who were regarded as the new holy family of Egypt. The pharaoh was considered half-divine and part of the living spirit of Aten. Amun's strength disappeared into oblivion. The atmosphere in Egyptian society became intense, with a high level of hostility between Akhenaten and the priestly class, the most powerful upper class.

In ancient Egypt, the priesthood was not only the most affluent but also the most influential group. These priests skillfully wielded both religious and political authority, contributing significantly to the nation's thriving economy through their control over precious resources and land. The Egyptians deeply believed that the watchful eye of Amun ensured their society's stability and that the gods played a pivotal role in driving their nation forward.

There were certain mysterious elements associated with the high priests. In many cases, the high priests revealed secrets of the unseen world and managed processions of important festivals. In return, the first fruits of the Earth were devoted as a sacred offering to support the priesthood.

Each religious statue possessed immense impact on people's everyday lives, with power held within them. These statues significantly contributed to the overall health of the economy through daily rituals, performances, and offerings that guaranteed safety and maintained life's balance as bestowed by the gods.

Before the rule of King Akhenaten, Aten was a relatively obscure and a lesser-known deity with minimal importance. People only had vague knowledge about Atenism, understanding that this god occupied a lower rank among the numerous divine entities in their universe.

Under Akhenaten, Aten was thought to be the power of nature and the source of life. The existence of all life forms was sustained by the disc and the brightness of the sun's rays. Amun became the lesser god associated with the underworld during the darkness of night.

Aten soared to prominence as the ultimate deity before becoming the sole recognized god throughout Egypt. As the closest embodiment of Aten, the pharaoh took on a divine status, often hailed as an earthly god who presided over judgment and granted devout followers' passage into the afterlife.

However, Akhenaten's devotion to Atenism placed him at odds with Thebes' devoted priests and their steadfast supporters. Tensions escalated in the town, leaving a palpable sense of danger and mounting threats aimed at Atenism's adherents.

The old spirit in Akhenaten vanished, and his spiritual rebirth proved the mysterious monolithic Aten had become supreme.

Amenhotep's elder sibling, Thutmosis, was destined for kingship but tragically lost his life in a chariot accident. The vizier believed divine intervention mercifully ended his suffering. With Thutmosis gone, their mother Tiye assumed control of the royal throne, ruling alongside her son Akhenaten until he came of age.

Growing up, young Prince Amenhotep IV didn't always enjoy the same reverence as the rest of his royal kin. In fact, family portraits featuring Amenhotep III and Queen Tiye exhibited only five children, deliberately excluding Amenhotep IV due to his uniquely elongated skull and striking appearance. But with Thutmosis's untimely demise, Amenhotep IV suddenly found himself next in line for Egypt's coveted throne.

Amenhotep IV thought this good fortune was due to his being favored by Aten, so he dedicated the rest of his life to the god. Amenhotep IV ascended to the throne and, shortly afterward, reduced the power of the priestly class along with their influence and wealth.

A powerful shift was taking place, aiming to sever ties between Aten's followers and Amun's priesthood. The movement sought to strip funding from the temples and priests devoted to Amun, while abandoning other traditional gods at the king's command. Frustrated crowds demonstrated the disapproval of ordinary citizens and priests towards Atenism.

Situated on the eastern bank south of Thebes, Tell el-Amarna took center stage between two mountains. This vibrant city hosted residential areas, workshops, palaces, and the magnificent Great Temple of Aten towards its north. Devoted to the radiant sun disc deity, Aten, it welcomed all citizens to join in worship.

The reaching rays of sunlight illuminated a certain part of Amarna at sunrise before the bright rays could reach the entire nation. The new capital city was divided into three main areas devoted to the mysterious monolithic cult of Aten.

The north city was an administrative district that contained the royal residence and government structure between the river and the high plateau on the eastern part of the Nile.

As the sun's warm rays touched the magnificent temples, it was believed they brought prosperity and blessings to Egypt. Akhenaten was convinced that adopting these fresh religious ideals would uplift the lower class, allowing Atenism to forge unity and attract an abundance of blessings from Aten.

Stone slabs that encompassed the city's boundary and carved statues of the royal family were embedded in the rocks at the north and south, encircling the mountainous landscape.

There were scenes depicting the royal family in vibrant details in a distinctive Cretan style. At the entrance to the Royal Wadi was the hieroglyphic symbol of Akhet, which represented the sun rising over the horizon of the capital city of Amarna.

Amarna was built using a high-tech architectural technique, creating an artistic revolution in Egypt. In the Amarna era, stone structures were built with smaller blocks and stronger mortar with decorated monasteries. Often fewer workers were used to build structures with smaller columns supporting temples' roofs. This new technique was used to erect temples, residences, royal palaces, and several zoos for the pharaoh and his famous wife, Nefertiti. Minoan artwork dominated the new city of Amarna.

The main street was the Royal Road, which passed through the south into the center of Amarna between the official palace and the royal estate. The road extended over a bridge and stretched into a square in front of the entrance fascia of the Great Temple.

In the heart of the city, two main temples were dedicated to Aten and surrounded by the royal administrative areas. The Great Temple of Aten served as the main place of worship in the new sacred city.

To the south were suburbs comprised of noble citizens living quarters, including those of the high priests of Aten and the viziers of Egypt.

The new royal city was stunning and perhaps greater than all of Egypt, and along with the king having a beautiful wife to enjoy it with. Amarna was one place in the nation where Akhenaten believed he would be free to worship Atenism and spend valuable time with his family. In a way, the move elevated his wife Nefertiti.

Nefertiti and her younger sibling Mutnodjmet were gifted with mesmerizing beauty, undeniable charisma, and majestic personalities. With her dark complexion, eye-catching necklaces, and lavish golden adornments, Nefertiti possessed the allure of a goddess during her youth. Her slender bronze figure, silky black hair, and mesmeric dark brown eyes captivated everyone's attention.

Though she embraced the Aten faith, Nefertiti's passion for dancing and entertaining crowds never waned, as her flawless beauty continued to draw admiration. Hailing from an influential family that groomed brides for royal marriages, Nefertiti exceeded expectations by becoming not just a royal wife but also the co-ruler of Egypt.

Nefertiti's younger sister became the Great Royal Wife of Horemheb, the last pharaoh of the Eighteenth Dynasty, who returned Egypt to polytheism after the Amarna Period.

The priests were loyal to the god of Amun, and the viziers closest to the pharaoh were suspicious of the heretic king who had changed his name to Akhenaten. His father, Amenhotep the Magnificent, led Egypt into unrivaled prosperity and artistic greatness.

As a child, young Akhenaten was captivated by the image of Aten – the sun god – while he played near the Nile. He grew up in awe of the sun's far-reaching rays and developed a deep reverence for Atenism. As his fascination evolved, it ignited a conflict between two spiritual forces of darkness that threatened to rip apart the entire nation.

Tensions escalated, making life in Egypt unbearable. The forces of darkness seized every chance to deepen divisions among the people. It wasn't long before resentment intensified as Pharaoh Akhenaten led a revolutionary transition from polytheism to monotheism. This change altered Egypt forever, as the new monotheistic religion spread across its territories.

The gods of the outer world seized the nation like a burning torch, their flames fanning bitterness and division repeatedly. Egypt found itself being pulled in opposite directions, torn between its traditional beliefs and the emerging monotheistic faith.

Numerous ambitious individuals professed their devotion to Aten in pursuit of power. They willingly traded their integrity for a coveted spot within the king's inner circle. In contrast, ordinary folks dared not question the king's rule. Ordinary folks were hushed by fear, being taught about faith to preserve a sense of sacredness. While the pharaoh was seen as divine, religion occasionally served as a means to acquire wealth and power.

Some religious leaders clung to Atenism symbolically, prepared to abandon it upon detecting any hint of vulnerability. It seemed as if a dark shadow loomed, with sunlight held captive within the night's gloom.

And yet, the priests' thirst for power persisted, leaving people with no alternative but to embrace Atenism or worship in silence. Egypt found itself ensnared by sinister forces from beyond, entrapped in a senseless illusion. The more they battled this darkness, the further the nation descended into chaos. Religious leaders were regarded as godly interpreters but were expected to appease the king. As Queen Mother Tiye persevered in her dedication, she brought offerings to the temple of Amun, and every time there was a feast, the devoted assembly chanted, "Amen," with utmost enthusiasm.

Akhenaten began taxing the old temples and moved the Egyptian court and 80,000 citizens out of Thebes. Corruption began to spread rapidly throughout the countryside.

No one was more cautious than Mutnodjmet, the daughter of one of the most trusted viziers in Egypt and sister to the recently crowned queen. The ladies, Nefertiti and Mutnodjmet, proved to be women of incredible beauty and influence. Their wise voices captured the hearts of Egypt while the country was going through turmoil.

In contrast to Nefertiti, her younger sister, Mutnodjmet, had no desire for power. Her name meant "Sweet one of the goddesses Mut," who was a prominent sky goddess and divine mother in ancient Egyptian mythology, as well as Amun's companion. The love affair between the Prince and Nefertiti before he was king turned out to be advantageous, making Mitanni Egypt's most powerful ally and diminishing Kiya's status as a minor wife.

Kiya experienced the fading of her royal standing and found it challenging to match the standards set by Nefertiti in the king's life. Undoubtedly, Nefertiti's life was distinct from hers in numerous ways. Although Kiya married the Pharaoh before Nefertiti entered the picture, the alliance with Mitanni played a pivotal role in elevating Nefertiti to the position of Great Royal Wife. Nefertiti, having been born into a world of politics, held valuable experience in decision-making firsthand.

Akhenaten was the leader who kept the legacy of Aten alive. Still, the charisma of Nefertiti and the wise counsel of Mutnodjmet brought dramatic changes across the nation. Egypt teetered on the brink of civil war as Akhenaten's isolationist policies caused alliances to crumble. Horemheb, the high priest and the pharaoh's most devoted general and childhood friend, championed the priesthood of Amun. Resisting the shift toward Aten worship, he privately warned the king of impending civil war and corruption, advocating for citizens' religious freedom.

Despite his opposition, Horemheb loyally supported Akhenaten's religious views to preserve Egypt's unity. However, the skeptical priests in Thebes publicly rejected the king's faith. Meanwhile, Nefertiti harbored political aspirations and hungered for power more than her devotion to Aten. As Aten's influence spread throughout Egypt, a mysterious fury escalated, exacerbating fears of disunity.

The Pharaoh and his advisors discussed political and religious matters in the royal chamber. Mutnodjmet turned to gaze at Nefertiti before she laughed nervously. She bowed her head after the king gave her a fiery glance.

"Silence!" the pharaoh shouted.

Nefertiti quickly looked at her sister and walked out of the Great Hall, saying, "Mut, give me a helping hand." Outside the hall, she continued, "Keep your negative feelings to yourself and make sure you never interrupt the king again, Mut."

Mutnodjmet relaxed her shoulders and then walked away. Nefertiti inhaled and went back into the chambers.

There was no love in Thebes, only the passionate support of the vizier, who invited the king's mother, Tiye, to talk to her son. She brought along the high priest of Amun as though the king's arrogance was a demon that could be cast away.

The pace of the meeting hung motionless with his faith committed to his one and only god, Aten. But Nefertiti kept things calm. She brought attention back to political matters.

Sometime later, Tiye left the king's palace returning to Thebes and leaving a cloud of darkness over Egypt.

Akhenaten was left with his most trusted advisors. As though he had grown even more courageous, he proclaimed the pharaoh and Queen was both priests and had godlike status through their devotion to Aten.

The king found himself captive by the almighty Aten, while Prince Moses devoted himself to the sole God of the Israelites. In Akhenaten's eyes, the sun god Aten took precedence due to the Israelites' subjugation in Egypt. He couldn't imagine any other form of worship. The king was convinced that Aten was the one true deity. Egypt was swept by the powerful currents of two towering faiths – Atenism and the Hebrew beliefs.

Predominantly, it was the king's viewpoint that resonated with most Egyptians. They all sought to serve a chosen god for protection, yet for the king, there stood only one deity deemed worthy of reverence.

In both cases, monotheism was moving the nation toward a higher level of worship that had no carved images hidden in the temples. It portrayed all other forms of polytheism as demonic spirits or demons.

There was no room for compromise. The two friends' customs and religious faiths collided. There was no freedom to worship as long as Akhenaten was king. Moses was beyond angry.

CHAPTER 10

Moses was greatly loved by the people of Egypt, and he'd often wondered what his place was in the kingdom. He knew he was more fortunate than other Israelites and watched their suffering with a heavy burden of grief. His heritage was the one thing Moses never forgot in all his years of living the life of a prince.

It felt as if his life was deceptive, or his forgetfulness caused the Israelites to suffer through hideous torture. With this in mind, he pushed past the gruesome memories and worked tirelessly to be beneficial when the time was right.

Prince Moses had always loved Egypt—even if the nation had grown to dislike the Israelites. He was in the best position to comfort his people and had decided it might be wise to lead them out of bondage, but he wasn't sure how.

Moses became nearly silent about his faith in serving the God of the Israelites. Trapped in a tough situation, Moses found himself powerless against Atenism and the enslavement of the Israelites. For a brief instant, he teetered on the brink of having his true identity exposed.

After all, the prince had been living with the dark secret of his heritage, so it was safer to remain silent. The cult of Aten brought dramatic changes into a society that previously had the freedom to serve any gods. Now things were about to change!

The people were unable to choose anything other than the faith of Aten. There was a taste of bitterness ushered into the nation by Greek settlers and the fifth heavens. Aten and Amun-Ra were pagans at their core and were brought to Egypt by invaders.

The country was on the verge of a civil war, and the king believed his faith in Aten would protect him from any uprising against the throne. The nation was full of disloyal citizens waiting to explode. Hostility was in the air like kindling waiting to burst into flames.

According to Akhenaten, the gleaming eyes of the sun rays were imperative to the functioning of the governance structure. The economy and the military were all due to the brightness of light extending from the sun's rays. The ideas of hard-working citizens who helped build Egypt to prominence were often overlooked.

His eyes were opened. The thought was never clearer to the pharaoh than at this moment. No one desired faith in Aten more than Akhenaten. The nation was finally liberated from Amun.

In this case, Akhenaten chose to accept a monotheistic religion but not the faith of Prince Moses.

Akhenaten lived a lifetime without revealing Moses's true identity. The pharaoh had a solitary bitterness and a strong desire to choose the right path for Egypt. For Moses, however, only one God reigned supreme, and Aten was among other polytheistic deities not to be worshipped.

Prince Moses exclaimed to Akhenaten, "The Israelites follow a single God, the Egyptians should do the same!"

"Are you really serious about this?" The king inquired.

The king shook his head in frustration, ignoring the prince's arrogance. Still, Moses stood fast with the king, staring him straight in his dark-brown eyes. An element of softness pierced the king's heart as he turned away.

He gestured wildly, turning back in the direction of Moses. He took a deep breath to compose himself. His eyes rolled viciously as his heart slowed.

A hissing sound came from the lips of the king. Akhenaten gazed at Moses with his eyes wide open.

The king slowly and silently walked toward Moses, stared at him momentarily, and then said, "Don't let anyone hear you talk this way, Moses. Not everyone is your friend. There are enemies everywhere!"

The king's words lashed out like the sting of a whip! The men's words whirled at each other like a merry-go-round, each speaking disgustedly. Moses turned to glare at the pharaoh.

For a brief moment, they faced each other with a death stare. The king frowned with anger; his eyes fixed on the prince. An ironic smile replaced the frown. The pharaoh didn't say a word.

The conversation got a little strange, but passion and sanity forced the king and Moses to question their every thought. For a moment, it seemed like the high-pitched voice wasn't the king. There were constant pauses while each traded insult. Moses knew perfectly well that too much double talk would get them nowhere. A chill flowed through him like a gasp of fresh air. Still, there was silence.

The king took a deep breath but stayed quiet for a moment. Without a word, there seemed to be a constant battle of awkward silence. The silence allowed fresh peace and respect to sift through every unspoken word.

The prince tried to put his every thought into words. In Moses' mind, the truth was too much for the king. The men were so wrapped up in emotion. They understood each other's feelings.

"From this point forward, you must remember that you were born an Israelite and you are still an Israelite," said the king. Never in his entire life had the prince been threatened with revealing his identity; however, not many have known anyway.

The king had carried this secret since childhood but swore it would remain among the royal family. This was the wrong time for the prince to be labeled an Israelite. The political risk was too great.

The prince, who didn't speak well in a heated argument, had to learn to control his pain and emotion.

Moses held his tongue, taking a moment to calm the rage that bubbled up inside. The malicious words uttered by the king echoed in his mind before dissipating. The prince inhaled deeply and pivoted to exit the room, but hesitated and glanced back at the king for a brief instant. Realizing nothing more could be said, he bowed gently. Still, Moses lingered there.

The king didn't approve of this kind of argumentative conversation. Still, Moses was one of his closest advisors and could calm a crowd, especially the Israelites, who the king knew wanted to rise against oppression.

Hostility had gotten them nowhere. The king glanced up, clinging to his every word.

He said, "When will you learn? By taking the pathway to Atenism, Aten will show you the one and only God. I renounced idols and the old ways of robbing the poor, seized power from the priests, and returned Egypt to prosperity by not conquering foreign land that didn't belong to us. I pledge peace to our neighbors, a gesture of eternal love."

The prince became so caught up in the heated exchange that the king called for a guard to escort Moses out of his presence. The prince turned away and hurried out like the king had pierced his heart with a fiery spike.

Fortunately, the king employed Nubian guards, as many within his inner circle had turned against him. Despite their differences, he still deemed Prince Moses a friend. The king rarely made an effort to appease his advisors, who remained more devoted to their nation than to Akhenaten. After all, the king and his advisors hadn't seen eye to eye since he renounced Amun-Ra.

The people had been engaged in war for so long that their entire economy hinged on conflict with their enemies. They were eager to protect Egypt until their last breath. They built numerous temples and tombs with the spoils of war, causing confusion when Akhenaten introduced an era of peace throughout the nation.

In the Amarna period, the artistic and spiritual renaissance unveiled much about the Israelites, even more so than the Egyptians. While the shadow of civil war hung over Egypt, Israel faced adversity due to their lack of devotion to Yahweh. Their true power lay in unwavering belief in the Creator. The Almighty Creator selected Israel as His chosen nation, yet allowed the Israelites to be diminished to a state of servitude.

Raised as a royal prince by Pharaoh's daughter, Asiya, Prince Moses possessed the potential to become king himself. Little did people know that he was born with Israelite blood. When Akhenaten confronted Moses and insisted that he and his advisors worship Aten, the prince boldly made a stand before the king and queen. He demanded the liberation of the Israelites from their oppressive forced labor.

Queen Nefertiti remained silent, her respect for Prince Moses evident in her compassionate gaze. She found herself captivated by their deep conversation; her voice replaced by a tender smile of understanding.

Her feelings regarding the release of the Israelites never changed. The Israelites were oppressed for no reason other than envy and a means for power. The Egyptians had become dependent upon the profits of free labor, and nothing the prince could say appeared to save the Israelites from the burden of the lash.

"Continue on, Moses," Akhenaten spoke with a hint of sorrow. Despite Moses's fervent appeal, the king remained unsettled, as if he were enduring the nagging voice of an annoying priest. Even though Moses held the status of a hero in Egypt and was sheltered from oppression under the living king's reign, his true respect and treatment were on par with a prince born into prestige.

At the royal palace, Moses could freely express his thoughts – a privilege bestowed only to Horemheb, the king's long-time confidant. Indeed, Akhenaten yearned for nothing more than unwavering loyalty to Aten and devoted public servants working tirelessly for Egypt's future.

Even so, it was challenging for the king to persuade the prince to turn in Aten's direction. Prince Moses never pretended to share the king's beliefs, but there was no grudge or silent hatred toward each other.

Prince Moses was a man who spent his whole life working to improve Egypt. He was always dependable, and considered a heroic leader, but a shadow of being an Israelite hung over him.

As each day passed, the deep secret became increasingly powerful. The idea of someone exposing his identity haunted him constantly, causing affection and gratitude towards the prince to vanish. Egypt found itself under the shadow of the fifth heaven's insanity, a beautiful dream turning into a dreadful nightmare. The nation was spiraling towards economic ruin and isolation.

The brewing civil unrest created an opportunity for Smenkhare, the king's younger brother, to be named co-ruler of the throne. The threat of the Pharaoh's assassination loomed day and night, while violence spread throughout the Mediterranean like an uncontrollable epidemic. This chaos was orchestrated by the fifth heavens in a bid to unleash a devastating storm fueled by a lust for blood.

It became clear that a civil war was imminent, and the danger of national rivalries threatened to send the country into turmoil. This sudden change became a curse. The people were forced to accept Aten's new political movement and faith. In a world where Akhenaten deemed everything everlasting under the radiant glow of Aten, things took an unexpected turn. Ay, the most loyal confidant of the pharaoh, vanished like a shadow in the dark, sparking unrest in the kingdom.

Tension brewed as mercenaries from Nubia were brought in to safeguard the ruler. By the king's side, Horemheb stood unwavering while many others left the royal abode. Amidst this chaos, only a handful of devoted servants remained steadfast in their loyalty to the monarch.

Some believed insanity had crept into the pharaoh's inner thoughts and made him too weak to be a king. Even the queen, Nefertiti, abandoned Akhenaten and became isolated in her North Riverside Palace. Everything seemed to be closing in on the king, but he remained loyal to his faith.

Within the harem palace, women were confined like domesticated creatures for the king's enjoyment. Access to the harem was granted solely by the king's permission, and Akhenaten frequently paid visits during his rule. The harem was led by his primary wife, Nefertiti, while his lesser wives also took up residence.

Despite being off-limits to ordinary folk, adventurous young guards would stealthily infiltrate the palace, facing possible death if the king uncovered their deeds. Yet, they relished in these taboo delights and kept their lips sealed. As night shrouded everything in darkness, the guards stealthily entered the harem palace, a place where the residents' dignity often suffered due to neglect and indifference. Carefully staying silent, they knew all too well the lethal repercussions if their actions were discovered.

Nefertiti shared a deep passion for Horemheb, and the esteemed Great Royal Mother, Tiye, concealed her mysteries to protect the royal throne. There was considerable acceptance surrounding the slave girls and their romantic partners during their times of intimacy. The Pharaoh's religious devotion to Aten overshadowed his desires, causing his passion to vanish.

Despite the Pharaoh's undying love for Nefertiti, the queen couldn't ward off feelings of jealousy. Oblivious to the other harem-girls, the king devoted his heart solely to Nefertiti. Yearning for affection, the women sought solace in one another to fulfill their desires. As passion and eroticism consumed them, it became the ultimate source of excitement within the North Harem Palace's confines.

Happiness seemed lost for those who turned away from Atenism. Some days were akin to living in a nightmarish underworld, as if life in Egypt had stopped entirely. Hearts weighed heavy, and Maat, the deity of truth and justice, shattered the balance of morality.

The mission of Akhenaten's novel faith was to serve Aten by promoting harmony and benevolence, traits often mistaken for weaknesses rather than marks of regal magnificence. Once upon a time, Egypt relied on individual deities overseeing the country's matters. In this new belief system, Aten embodied both good and evil as a sign of divine affection.

The royal throne was taken over by a strategic plot designed by the fifth heavens. This was a new identity with an evil twist. Thebes had become a wicked city with a thirst for wealth and fame.

The dignity of Egypt was almost gone, and the king's most loyal supporters went along in the hope they'd attain access to the throne's power. The king's enemies outnumbered his allies while he promoted this new beacon of love that burnt like an eternal flame.

Each day brought the growing certainty that Akhenaten would lose his throne. As days turned darker, an enigmatic fury surged within the hearts of these untamed men, rebelling against Atenism. They hungered for revenge.

A feeling of desperation grew as the radical religion of Aten swept across the nation. It seemed Akhenaten suffered a curse of the blasphemy of his ruling. There was no escaping the curse.

The king had been living in delusion. His role was filled with deception, and he lived the life of an illusionist, breaking away from the priests to limit their increasing influence. Akhenaten's devotion to Aten formed a triad. The royal couple became religious heretics.

The king and his nation were moving in opposite directions. There was a touch of insanity in the atmosphere, enough to set the nation on fire. Egypt was filled with venom.

As time passed, Nefertiti's frustration grew to an appalling silence. Nefertiti came to her senses and left the royal palace with no desire to return to her role as the queen.

Perhaps the pregnancy of Kiya played a vital role in nudging Nefertiti to relinquish her position as the Great Royal Wife. In Kiya's perspective, Nefertiti transformed into a desolate, pitiful queen who no longer had anything significant to offer.

Akhenaten's mind was clouded by his actions towards the high priest of Amun, leading him to worry about potential revenge and struggle with conspiracies planning his demise. To ensure peace and establish divine credibility for Aten as the life-giver, Akhenaten made strategic decisions that fostered amicable relations with neighboring nations.

The arrival of the new capital ushered in an era of magnificent temples, shrines, and artistic masterpieces that seemed like divine blessings. However, the introduction of Atenism deviated from the norm and was implemented too rapidly for people to fully embrace it as their sole faith.

Things were going so badly in the new holy city of Amarna that Nubian guards were more trustworthy than the royal security forces. Something was bound to happen.

The sun burned brightly while the unruly crowd tried to enter the palace gates, and others attempted to scale the palace walls. Rumors were growing louder in the depths of the palace, and the emotions were a constant reminder of an insurgency for Amun.

An enraged mob marched through the streets, slowly making their way past the palace gates. They bellowed terrifying threats aimed at the king. A powerful animosity towards the ruler permeated the air, and one could feel the religious turmoil between the cults of Amun and Aten. It was as though an insidious madness had fallen upon the nation, fueled by the sun's scorching rays and sparking a rebellious spirit.

Previously, Amun stood as the paramount deity in their polytheistic religion, but now Aten had risen to supremacy, replacing all other gods. With Aten crowned as Egypt's sole divine being, Akhenaten assumed his role as Aten's son, governing Earth with guidance from the sun's radiance. Thus, Akhenaten set himself apart from those who came before him, embracing his title as "The Son of the Sun-God Aten."

King Akhenaten transformed into a living embodiment of his deity, known as "The Beautiful Child of Aten." A magnificent monument was erected, showcasing massive sculptures of Akhenaten and Queen Nefertiti, honoring the sun disc.

In a way, the king's dominion became an unbearable prison supported by greed and a power structure created to eliminate all the priests of Thebes.

In a twist of fate, people forsook their faith to gain power within Egypt's new regime. The overwhelming influence of Amun was inescapable, delivering a crushing blow to the nation. This shift signified a transformation sweeping across the Egyptian Empire. The nation grew increasingly hostile and unruly, showing little respect for the royal throne and shrouded in turmoil as anger permeated throughout.

Despite popular opinion, Akhenaten remained Egypt's Pharaoh, holding immense power in the Mediterranean region. Nefertiti stood by his side, proclaiming her belief in Aten's monotheistic teachings until she left the palace. The door opened for Egyptians to fight back and reclaim their lands so they could return to their self-indulgent ways. The people were left with a choice: follow the god Amun or embrace Aten's unfamiliar faith.

Amun-Ra and the radiant sun disc, Aten, were brought to Egypt by Greek settlers and warmly embraced by the Egyptians as part of their own culture. It was indeed a spiritual invasion by unseen forces of darkness. The fifth heavens had turned Egypt into a heathen nation.

The vision Akhenaten had for Egypt had been slowly beginning to fade away. The reality of civil war became increasingly imminent. Political clout grew with patriotism fading into resistance.

Deception and malice lingered over the nation, blowing a taste of bitterness in the air. Somehow, this anger arose, changing the political, cultural, and economic environment between the elites.

Some of the elites were driven into poverty and misery. Those who refused to change their allegiance to Aten, the sun disc, were sentenced to death by the sword.

Akhenaten's dream had turned into a nightmare. Frustration filled his soul with madness. He became helpless with a sudden sickness. The sun darkened his skin and the pupils in his eyes were like a prowling beast.

The king fell ill with pneumonia and depression, enough to bedbound him to the palace.

He was like a drunken man possessed by an evil curse. His sickness revealed itself in the form of madness. His happiness had gone away, and in a panic, he struggled with pain that was too great to endure.

Then word went out that Meryre, the high priest and chief prophet, was run out of the palace by Horemheb, the chief of security. Meryre was once the High Priest of Aten and served as a fan-bearer and the king's closest spiritual advisor.

It was as if the king couldn't free himself from his nightmare and the crudeness of a bad dream. There was no sanity there.

Gradually, servants of the temple noticed his mind slipping into deep insanity. His voice was brittle and low, as if his tongue was reluctant to reveal his loss of sanity.

The Pharaoh knew he was dying as a flash of fear flowed through his mind. He hoped to ease the image of death. He was lost in thought and cursed by confusion.

Everything was going wrong for him. The first sign of panic came from within his inner circle. Everyone played a part in his demise.

It felt like everyone, from his foes to his advisors, conspired against him. The gods had sided firmly with his adversaries. Absent was justice, replaced by an insatiable thirst for power surrounding him.

His brown eyes glimmered with humorless passion as he gazed around the room in total sadness. His one and only god, Aten, had forsaken him in his moment of destiny.

The voice of Aten was silent. The pain of a broken heart penetrated his very soul, and death stared him straight in the face.

It seemed his destiny was connected to his faith in the god who had betrayed him for some unknown reason. This was his world, a time of isolation, illness, and a period of sudden anguish amid strange nightmares.

The bright rays of Aten dimmed with the enchantment of the cold breeze of winter, which snatched the beauty of sunlight away from the fortress on the western side of the Nile.

The Pharaoh broke into a cold sweat, his mind carrying him away from consciousness. Aten's flaming torch became a nightmare and invaded Egypt with pure bitterness on a grand scale of vengeance.

The reaching rays of Aten blazed in daylight and then suddenly spun a degree of blindness throughout the Mediterranean.

The night sky shone enough to quench the hostility outside the palace. A lot of gossip claimed the pharaoh was dying and his mind was slipping away in total darkness.

Uneasy mockery and insults were rushing through the air without much fighting. After, there was more sympathy due to the king's sickness.

None of that mattered enough to quell the crowd's anger. The nation was in pain and waiting in desperation as the shadow of the midnight sky stretched over the horizon.

Whispers spread that the mysterious silhouette of Anubis—the dog -headed deity of death who safeguarded spirits—cast its presence over the royal residence. As daylight broke, the assembly started to recite songs in honor of Osiris, the divine judge of the underworld who brought renewal through nature's never-ending cycles, nourished by the Nile's bountiful flow. Intense emotions filled the atmosphere while a wave of skepticism swept across the African heavens.

Akhenaten dropped the funeral service of Osiris in favor of Aten, the life-giving and sustaining power of the sun.

The pharaoh's role had become a source of blessings after death. Nefertiti shared the king's celestial role. There were rumors that Nefertiti annulled the festival of the Nile commemorating Osiris's guardian of death and rebirth in favor of Aten. Atenism replaced all graven images.

Even on his deathbed, Akhenaten refused to compromise his faith. His sudden change in health tested his loyalty to Aten, who the king was determined to worship daily.

The king recovered enough to tilt his shoulders upward with his eyes fixed toward the window. He was beginning to breathe again and was taking fresh gasps of air. There was a lot of speculation, but the king swiftly straightened up and got out of bed.

There was something inside of him that gave him the strength to come alive. His eyes seemed full of misery amid his sickness. There was no insight into his thoughts. His face was absorbed with confusion.

His appearance gave the servants chills. His shoulders slumped forward while his feet dangled from his frail weakness.

Finally, he slowly lifted himself and stood along the bed while the guard watched silently. He crept forward.

The king sluggishly paced toward the window with a Nubian guard looking from a distance on the other side of the room. He found the ability to make his way to the window to glance toward the sun.

"Good morning, Your Highness," said the guard.

The king's face gleamed with excitement, but he was breathless. For a moment, he stood there shivering in silence.

Then, the king stared out the window, looking for the sun's golden rays for comfort, only to see scattered clouds blocking the divine rays. He tried to grasp an explanation for his sickness.

His silhouette before the window appeared frail to the spectators. The crowd continued to sing hymns while the king stood in the window. From a distance, the crowd could see the image of the king with his fragile stature leaning forward as he trembled silently.

The king heard the wailing voices of the crowd as he turned away to face his final destiny. The guard rushed over quickly, lifted the king's arms, and grabbed his waist so that the king could find his way back to his bed.

He dragged his feet with his head down toward the floor. His world had turned dark, and his spirit seemed to fade to a strange place. Akhenaten slowly paced back to his bed with a splash of life, too weak to argue his fate. There was no real hurry. He was breathless old, sick man without royal power. He seemed lucky to be alive.

He couldn't hide the pain in his eyes. His doubts of sanity were drowned out by grief for his faith in Aten.

His frail body told it all. The truth was obvious; he'd become terrified and was uncertain of anything around him. He was still tall and slim and had a slow, painful, clumsy walk.

The king's loyalty to his god was deeper than his love for his country. The people silently accepted that the god, Amun, cursed the king, and he'd slipped into insanity. He spent most of his last days in complete solitude.

Outside the palace, a sense of mockery filled the air. A surge of indignant anger toward the king, accompanied by menacing taunts, permeated the atmosphere.

At the sight of death, they all abandoned him or chased his loved ones away, attempting to rid Egypt of the king's influence. The god he loved so much and sacrificed his throne for had deceived him.

The curse of the fifth heavens sent him sweet dreams of power, but it quickly became a nightmare. In addition, his divine status had come to an end!

The fifth heavens had successfully introduced paganism and idolatry into Egypt. The journey was superstitious, and a plan to push the nation into paganism vanished in a sudden silence, just like the rays of sunlight.

In an instant, the king was gone! His soul was finally ripped away. His life vanished like a stroke of lightning. He was summoned into the clouds by the gods of the outer world.

CHAPTER 11

THE RAVING MOB BECAME silent when Horemheb, the security chief, announced the pharaoh was dead. "The royal falcon has flown to heaven."

The chaotic crowd was torn between cheering and mourning the king's demise. Despite being a benevolent ruler, his death left an uneasy atmosphere. A fleeting gust whispered across the kingdom, hinting at newfound loyalty to Amun and whispering fears of Egypt's collapse. The nation seemed vulnerable, with a neglected military adding to the turmoil.

Horemheb quickly performed his duty as general and chief of security of the royal family. Horemheb ordered the guards to stay close to the royal family and sent armed guards to close in around Nefertiti and her daughters at the Northside Palace. The queen's younger sister, Mutnodjmet, was also returned to the palace.

Amidst an intense conflict with Mitanni in Northern Syria, the Hittites caught wind of the king's demise and swiftly deployed their forces to Egypt's border, brandishing threats of invasion. Akhenaten's palace was teeming with foreign guards, as the ruler had employed Ethiopian and Nubian protectors. Horemheb, however, lacked faith in the hired hands and demanded that all foreign guards clear out from Amarna, the capital city.

With great emphasis on proper protocol and respect for the throne, he issued clear directions. Upholding the governing body's sovereignty was crucial, and his authoritative demeanor was unmistakable. Horemheb, the determined general, called upon Smenkhare from Memphis and Ay, the high-ranking official from Thebes. It was crucial to avert power struggles that could destabilize the nation. Despite being a fierce warrior, Horemheb hoped to avoid plunging Egypt into a devastating civil conflict.

It was an era of allegiance, yet unrest and potential conflict lurked beneath the surface. The nation required a skilled leader who could restore Egypt's loyalist control without sparking panic or street revolts. When Nefertiti journeyed from the Northside Palace to the Royal Palace, General Horemheb greeted her warmly, with Mutnodjmet at her side.

There was a moment of silence before the general said, "Welcome home, your Majesty."

Everyone was cheering for her return and refrained from judgment—at least until the seat of governance was firmly in place.

Nefertiti was still consumed with grief from the death of her daughter during childbirth, and the death of Princess Meketaten, her second eldest daughter. Nefertiti was brought back to the palace with her four daughters, but it was hard to collect her thoughts amidst her grief. She tried to stay calm and sensible.

There was a moment when Mutnodjmet tried to make sense of the sudden certainty that seemed to be driving her out of her mind. There was so much attention on Nefertiti and Mutnodjmet. She looked down and glimpsed at every footstep while walking toward the palace.

The humid air echoed with the cheering crowd, gradually seeping into her thoughts. Her royal status was filled with some danger.

The people had grown wild and weary in the streets of Egypt, but Nefertiti was still adored; she was loved and respected. Perhaps she was the only one who could calm an unruly crowd. Mutnodjmet was rushed into the royal palace, surrounded by armed guards, passing through the cheering crowd.

She dodged the hailing crowd, who wanted just the slightest touch. Mutnodjmet wanted to drop her head out of shame from having the armed guards around her.

She was whisked into the palace with alarming speed, surrounded by a seemingly excessive number of guards. They pushed through the throngs of people, moving quickly under the golden sunlight, while armed protectors kept vigilant watch in the glistening break of day. Mutnodjmet found herself lost in thought.

Never did she believe she held such significance. Perhaps Nefertiti possessed nobility, but Mutnodjmet struggled to recognize her own prominence as she observed the emotional crowd – some shedding tears and others loudly praising Amun-Ra.

She chose to ignore her sister Nefertiti's anxiety and the nearby general. His sword was poised at his right hand, casually resting on his hip. It was evident that Nefertiti was struggling to find her voice.

Nefertiti's lips desperately sought the appropriate words as her breaths became ragged. To the onlookers, she embodied perfection amidst this somber occasion. In reality, she fought back the urge to sob uncontrollably.

Amidst the chaos, the two sisters struggled to find moments together, yet exchanged wistful, melancholy smiles. Mutnodjmet could sense her sister's unease as Nefertiti mustered the strength to make life-altering choices. She brushed away her tears, swallowing her sorrow and remaining silent.

Prince Moses embarked on a mission to halt the encroaching Hittites from invading Egyptian lands. The sudden arrival of Moses with a massive cavalry amidst the rugged terrain struck fear into the Hittites' hearts. They retreated at the first hint of looming danger.

Once the risk of war diminished, Egyptians rediscovered their unity and felt bound by their shared love for their country. Everything seemed surreal, like a dream. The unseen hand of Amun-Ra reached into the royal palace before vanishing abruptly, leaving behind deceitful misery. With every turn, circumstances changed rapidly, and now the future of Egypt hung in the balance.

Throughout his life, Akhenaten found himself constantly challenged by Horemheb's troublesome illusions and power-hungry individuals circling him like vultures. Despite his struggle for absolute control, a position even the gods couldn't sustain, Akhenaten sought to bridge the gap between the common people and the pharaoh. He grew increasingly skeptical of the priesthood's intentions.

Upon his death, a tense calm settled over the nation. Deep down, Nefertiti felt it unwise to involve Smenkhare in ruling the kingdom. Her instincts warned her of the dangers in sharing power with him, but she tried to dismiss such thoughts. It was evident that she harbored no love for Smenkhare.

Tensions still simmered among Akhenaten's followers after he appointed Smenkhare as co-ruler of Egypt to satisfy Amun's demands. Nefertiti desperately fought her doubts, as Egypt's future hung in the balance.

Nefertiti's fury blazed within her, her expression revealing the tale. As if signaling hope, the clouds momentarily dispersed along the skyline. Her resentment faded as Sage Ay, her father, arrived in Amarna. Before Nefertiti could utter a word, Mutnodjmet sprinted through the throng to embrace him. She dashed with tear-filled eyes and a yearning for his wise advice during these trying times. Stunned, he hugged his daughter while Nefertiti joined them in the tender moment.

In life, Akhenaten sought to appease Aten; now, reaching accord between Amun and Egypt hinged on their shifting power dynamics. Meanwhile, the deities of the fifth heavens cunningly observed.

As the wind swept across the empire, the moon dipped below the horizon, leaving darkness in its wake. A foreboding voice from beyond echoed throughout the Nile, sowing discord among its people.

Akhenaten, the infamous heretic king, met a tragic end, consumed by sorrow. In the afterlife, he faced judgment by Osiris – the lord of the underworld who presided over his eternal trial. Upon his verdict, Akhenaten's spirit was set free to journey beyond for Osiris's final decision.

The king's utopian vision for Egypt dissipated like mist, absorbed into the earth. With his time on earth complete, bitter disappointment smothered his dream of a harmonious nation. Hatred united the gods against this once mighty kingdom, leaving the Egyptians too feeble even to lament their fate.

The enigmatic gods from realms beyond had sown a formidable seed of animosity. This sinister rift swiftly engulfed the nation. Both Egyptians and Israelites were caught in the crosshairs of celestial forces from the fifth heavens, intent on reducing them to insignificance. Deepening divisions within the nation's heart presented ample opportunities for exploitation.

The differences between Egyptians and Israelites extended far beyond skin color. Their once-shared divine beliefs diverged, and their cultures evolved into barely recognizable forms. They found themselves drifting in opposite directions.

A whirlwind of transformation swept the nation, bringing with it an undercurrent of bitterness that tore apart the very fabric of society through a heinous act of terror. Unbeknownst to them, an invisible force had manipulated their hearts with seeds of discord.

A revolution in the artistic realm spurred Akhenaten to abandon obsolete ideologies. He dreamt of establishing a new city dedicated to serving Aten, his one and only god. Whether Aten accepted or disapproved of his actions remains uncertain; nonetheless, Akhenaten cast aside idols and banished Greek settlers from Egyptian soil.

Motivated by Aten's perceived desires, Akhenaten embarked on constructing a grand royal city, looting Thebes for its splendor to please the sun disc deity. These pagan gods of the fifth heavens were like unseen soldiers fighting against the Egyptian Empire in every way possible.

The gods of the fifth heavens rejected the heathen city like Atlantis. Perhaps the pharaoh didn't know the same rules applied in Egypt as it did Atlantis and Crete. The spiritual gods of the fifth heavens were working to destroy the whole system of the Mediterranean. The invisible gods were on a path of vengeance, and the result would be disastrous in Egypt.

The nation fell into savage cynicism. There was no light at the end of the tunnel. It was as though the sun had faded into darkness. The curse of the fifth heavens rolled out like furious balls of fire in all directions.

Atenism filled a vacuum of divisiveness that suggested divine forces were moving in the lower heavens around the earth. The gods of the outer world used human weakness to gain supernatural strength. It was a mysterious power hovering above the horizon with the taste of blood. The fifth heavens wanted to send horrendous atrocities upon the Hebrew-speaking people and for them to kneel at the statues representing supremacy.

When the divine rays of the sun emerged above the fields, they nourished the rich black soil of Egypt and made the land perfect for growing crops.

The sun's rays glowed as rain brought continuous water supply to the Mediterranean and the Red Sea. The water flowed from the Ethiopian Highland into the gifted river Nile. The nation was blessed with an abundance of resources.

The idea that all living pharaohs were incarnations of gods and carried out secular duties by performing religious rituals was passed on. These fundamentals of the universe were believed to maintain a balance of truth that revolved around a divine pharaoh.

The Graeco-Hyksos were polytheistic and believed in a variety of gods as well as demonic spirits, both good and bad.

The might of the Graeco-Hyksos struck more fear into the hearts of the Egyptians than their own physical prowess. As panic intensified, it felt as if time itself was slowing. Countless lives were lost in pursuit of the elusive fifth heavens, an unseen enemy to the Egyptians. It was a never-ending nightmare, with memories that refused to fade and minds ensnared in an endless whirlpool.

Shadowed by a deep and moral darkness, the Egyptian civilization suffered. The pharaohs, priests, and governing structures all became mere puppets controlled by an unstoppable force driving the nation through a cosmic battle.

Though they escaped physical enslavement, the Egyptians could not break free from the spiritual chains binding them to the lesser world of the fifth heavens. Their once-great empire was diminished, manipulated by unseen forces in the shadows of this feared realm.

In a sense, the Egyptians found themselves held captive by the unyielding pagan gods, blind to the suffering of their own people. It was as if the fifth heavens cast a malicious shadow upon both the Egyptians and the Israelites, driving a permanent wedge between them.

A new ruler, Smenkhare, ascended to the throne, accompanied by a cadre of soldiers. This shift in power ignited fierce competition among Egypt's governing factions. All around them, a fresh conflict began to stir. And just like that, changes swept through Egypt – most notably, people regaining the freedom to worship their ancestral gods.

Amun, the hidden one, was banned by Akhenaten, who dramatically shifted the religion and culture of freedom away from polytheism. Aten was the god of life-giving light rays and remained absent during nightfall before being resurrected in the early dawn.

Amun was the religion of the elites and brought wealth to the upper class. Much of the revenue of the Temple of Amun had been eroded, and traditional temples closed when Akhenaten abandoned the city of Thebes for his new capital in Amarna.

Prior to Akhenaten's reign, the priesthood wasn't particular about the polytheistic gods they worshipped or the unique rituals for their followers. Religion was a personal affair, and people choose their own ways to honor their deities.

During Akhenaten's time, he revolutionized the religious landscape by discarding the worship of numerous gods, images, and statues. Instead, he introduced a monotheistic belief system centered around Aten, the sun disc, who would grant blessings through its rays.

This groundbreaking shift rocked the foundation of the priesthood and left religious zealots speechless. Accused of heresy, many labeled Akhenaten as a self-proclaimed deity. The consequences were severe for those who didn't adapt, leading to their mass departure from Thebes.

Aten's novel monotheistic doctrine swiftly spread throughout Egypt, eclipsing polytheistic worship and causing the abandonment of old gods. Akhenaten branded them as superstitions and deemed them off-limits – a world that emerged from turmoil and strife.

However, during the end of the New Kingdom era, Smenkhare sought to restore balance by guiding Egyptians back to their local gods. He successfully resurrected traditional religious freedom that had existed before Akhenaten's rule.

In a perplexing turn of events, Smenkhare granted religious freedom in some areas of Egypt, but took a stricter stance in Memphis.

There, he targeted and executed followers of Amun while desecrating the Amun temples in Thebes. He held Amun-Ra accountable for Akhenaten's misfortune. Shifting the royal administration to Memphis, the Old Kingdom capital, Nefertiti governed Upper Egypt.

Before departing Amarna, Smenkhare married Nefertiti's eldest daughter, Meritaten, who took on the responsibilities of Great Royal

Wife or Chief Queen. This strategic marriage mirrored common practices within Egyptian royalty to maintain power. Despite this, Egypt experienced continuous violence against the Israelites and began a reconstruction effort to restore its grandeur. This tumultuous period incited hostility and social upheaval.

Foreign captives from Nubia, Palestine, and Israel were employed, amassing significant wealth and introducing new ideas, as well as providing labor for temple construction and monument building. Fueled by unwavering determination, Smenkhare focused on restoring damaged temples and mending broken alliances with former allies.

As more slaves succumbed to the exhausting workload, tensions heightened between Prince Moses and those supervising these harsh tasks.

The Israelites endured enslavement from dawn until dusk with little respite. They provided food and labor to the Egyptians, who exhibited no empathy towards them. Egypt's entire economy was dependent on Israelite labor, while the ruling elite lived leisurely lives.

CHAPTER 12

THE PRINCE WATCHED AS the Israelite's burden became heavier. Moses had become more powerful and closer to the throne than ever before. Now, only Nefertiti and Smenkhare stood in the way of Moses becoming king. As mistreatment increased, outrage from Moses morphed into a wave of fierce anger.

To Moses, the Israelites were more than just ordinary enslaved people. They were the chosen people of a new covenant. Prince Moses achieved power and authority but had great compassion for the Israelites.

Moses scoffed at the soldiers as they pressured the servant to work harder. His eyes burned with fury as he stormed towards the guard, ready to confront him.

"How dare you treat people like this!" Moses exclaimed.

The guard retorted, "They're just ordinary slaves, and I'm following orders to increase their workload."

Prince Moses stiffened and demanded, "Kneel before me. This is no way to boost workflow."

The guard refused to listen. The soldier was bold with his words and dared to look Moses straight in the eye.

The tension from the heated confrontation reached a boiling point. Swiftly, the prince unsheathed his sword, its razor-sharp edge striking the soldier with immense force. As the guard's throat was cut, his blood cascaded onto the sandy ground. His body slumped lifelessly, collapsing to the earth.

Moses stood paralyzed as his anger morphed into overwhelming dread. A servant watched this scene unfold from afar but was too fearful to intervene.

Bleeding profusely, the soldier's life hung by a thread as he desperately clung to existence. He tried to inhale but found no air. With an exhalation that seemed to touch the heavens, he took his final breath.

Undeterred, the prince delivered another powerful attack as the dying guard struggled for oxygen. Moses' swift strike ensured the soldier's demise.

The prince dropped the sword as if it had become hot metal and as if he had seen a demon in its purest form. The demon vanished with an ironic smirk.

The soldier died as the servant looked on in horror and panic. Moses shook his head in a bit of confusion. He took a deep breath to calm his frantic thoughts.

The servant was staring and too afraid to move. For a moment, their eyes locked, fixed on each other with confusion.

The servant's thoughts were vividly displayed on his face. How could a prince slay a soldier just to protect an enslaved individual? His eyes bulged in shock, and his breathing grew heavy with dread. Astonishment seized the servant, while Moses' radiant aura gradually diminished. Gazing into the servant's fearful eyes, Moses stood in silence. With fear about the king's potential reaction, the servant maintained a cautious distance from the prince, his eyes brimming with fear and unease.

Prince Moses pressed his finger to his lips for a vow of secrecy, then waved his hand for the servant to flee.

The servant bowed his head in agreement while a flash of fear settled on his face. The two exchanged knowing nods, but the servant's unwavering loyalty to his tyrannical ruler led him to display a hint of defiance. He inhaled deeply, turned his back, and uneasily left the vineyard, unable to shake the gruesome, vivid image that haunted his mind.

Fighting his nerves, he conveyed the news to Smenkhare – a man who held no regard for Moses as a prince. Smenkhare was constantly worried that Moses might succeed the throne due to his adoption into the royal family, a prospect that left him deeply displeased.

Although Prince Moses possessed power, authority, and a notable standing under King Akhenaten's rule, his once beloved king was no more. As for Moses, he remained silent, his sanity dissipating with each passing moment. The haunting image clung to him like a lingering nightmare.

An erratic fear troubled his thoughts as he wrestled with his emotions. The prince's brown eyes clouded with rage as drops of water formed on his brow.

It seemed his every thought had become destructive. He was desperate to bring his doubts and fears to some end. His temper became predominantly worse with every passing minute.

The prince had changed. Damnation had been too much for him. His life looked hopeless. This wasn't supposed to happen. His ill temper had finally left him empty and cold.

The prince's sanity had rapidly deteriorated. Smenkhare deemed the guard's slaying unforgivable. In the blink of an eye, everything shifted. His entire world plunged into a deep, dark abyss, yet he refused to acknowledge the stinging burn of defeat. Despite this, he fought to rid himself of the haunting memories that cast a shadow over his life.

An overwhelming urgency weighed heavily on his heart, draining his energy. He lost control of his life, desperately trying to free his mind from madness. Thoughts of escape brought forth a crippling weakness like never before.

Egypt – the land he loved so dearly – would never be the same for him. Astonishingly swift was his fall from power. As he closed his eyes briefly, a fleeting sense of calm washed over him, slightly alleviating his tormented disposition.

He glanced up in silence as though he were somehow relieved of his inner thoughts. His face glowed with violence as if anger had siphoned away his sanity.

He was angry and afraid, and his character swiftly changed from betrayal to the need for a sudden escape. He was frail with weakness. He fought the waves of a changing tide to survive the wrath of Smenkhare.

Smenkhare gave his soldiers orders to escort the prince back to Memphis. There was an epic hunt for Prince Moses, and Smenkhare boldly participated.

Everything else became of secondary importance to Smenkhare's command. Nothing could change his mind. The soldiers immediately began the hunt.

Upon discovering the plan to capture him, Moses hastily fled towards the desert, journeying relentlessly through day and night. He skillfully evaded the Egyptians by steering clear of public roads, hoping to escape Egypt's wrath. Haunted daily by Smenkhare's forces, the prince could find no way to mend the situation.

Prince Moses' life had taken an unexpected turn – from a luxurious royal existence in Egypt to running away from the very place he called home. Feeling utterly helpless, his heart threatened to give out at any moment. The relentless pounding in his chest and rivers of sweat were bad enough, but Moses couldn't shake the thought of fleeing through the night on horseback, from city to desert, in search of safety.

As the pursuit intensified and his strength waned, Moses knew he must forge ahead. The chase consumed him, instilling pure terror in his heart. Driven by fear, he moved faster than ever, accompanied only by the resounding thunder of his horse's galloping hooves. Eventually, as the furious sun gave way to darkness, Moses managed to leave his pursuers far behind and escape their grasp.

Under the moonlit sky, he raced ahead, trying to keep a distance from the thundering hooves of pursuing horses. The desert was unforgiving, with searing heat during the day and pitch-black nights. It presented a treacherous path with wild creatures lurking in its shadows.

As exhaustion overwhelmed him, a spark of hope ignited within, allowing fear to transform into courage. With newfound strength, he surged forward like a bolt of lightning. Prince Moses grappled with the harsh desert elements while seeking his freedom, haunted by the wrath of soldiers who sought to bring him to a deadly trial.

Feeling feverish chills, he couldn't tell if it was the heat or the constant reminder of his isolation that brought fear upon him. Stripped of his royal status and struggling to survive, he faced many tearful and sleepless nights. Yet, Moses refused to let despair get the better of him; he had to muster his strength to overcome both physical and mental barriers.

The unbearable heat took its toll on his spirit as relentless pursuers kept up their steady pace. Escape from the vengeful men seemed impossible. But in this arid wasteland with no guarantee of safety, every breath became a miracle—a new chance at survival.

Trapped in an unending cycle of insanity, Prince Moses battled loneliness and exhaustion. But despite these challenges, he knew that his pursuit for freedom had to go on.

Humbly, Prince Moses prayed and made offerings to the Creator, seeking protection from the wrath of the Egyptians. Meanwhile, Smenkhare eagerly joined the pursuit, demanding his troops to capture Moses and display his head on a stake.

The soldiers' fervor intensified as they chanted like ravenous animals, driven by madness. Anxiety engulfed the Royal Palace in Amarna when news of the prince's pursuit reached its walls.

"The soldiers will kill Moses at first sight," Horemheb warned. Nefertiti's anger boiled over as she yelled, *"A beast now sits on Egypt's throne!"* In an attempt to mediate the situation, she gestured to the

divided soldiers – some pounding their chests for vengeance, others shedding tears in loyalty to Prince Moses. The air was thick with unrelenting tension as they sought justice.

Nefertiti glared at Horemheb, remarking, "Smenkhare should show more respect than to chase a beloved prince like prey." She couldn't believe it – the potential capture of the prince overshadowed everything else in Egypt. This went beyond a simple guard's murder in a vineyard.

The rising popularity and royal status of the prince posed a threat to Smenkhare's claim to the throne. In response, she dispatched a delegation to Ethiopia, requesting safe passage for Prince Moses. As they waited, they did their best to ignore any negative thoughts about the prince's escape.

Nefertiti's expression turned somber as she remarked, "The Ethiopian has given asylum to many people fleeing for safety." Smenkhare, however, had already made up his mind to end Moses's life without giving him an opportunity to defend himself. Smenkhare struggled to contain his emotions—his determination fueled by a deeper hostility towards the prince and driven by a bloodlust in his role as king.

In Amarna, Moses was adored, but the Israelites remained shackled. Nefertiti directed her prayers towards Aten and her late husband Akhenaten, hoping for their guidance from the afterlife.

> "Thou arisest fair in the horizon of Heaven,
> O living Aten, Beginner of life.
> When thou dawnest in the East,
> thou fillest every land with beauty.
> Thou art comely, great, radiant, and high over every land.
> Thy rays embrace the lands to the full extent of all that
> thou hast made, for thou, art Re and attain their limits and subduest
> them for thy beloved son, Akhenaten."

The audience chambers centered on Nefertiti as if Aten, the reaching rays of the sun god, could hear her prayers. The echo of her voice lingered in the room. She continued to pray:

"And the lands of Syria, Kush, and Egypt—
thou appointest every man to his place and satisfy his needs.
Everyone receives his sustenance, and his days are numbered.
Their tongues are diverse in speech and qualities likewise,
and their color is differentiated for thou hast
distinguished the nations.

Thou makest waters under the earth, and thou bringest
them forth at thy pleasure to sustain the people of Egypt
even as thou hast made them live for thee,
O Divine Lord of them all, toiling for them,
the Lord of every land, shining forth for them,
the Aten disc of the day-time, great in majesty!"

CHAPTER 13

PRINCE MOSES'S WORLD WAS getting smaller, and he had nowhere to hide from the wrath of Smenkhare. His world was filled with darkness. The prince was forced to wrestle with his new loneliness. It was becoming increasingly hard to process his inner thoughts. He knew at any moment; the angry mob could end his life.

The sun rose higher, fading from the quiet breeze of moonlight.

There was perfect silence as if time had come to a halt.

The prince had become like Akhenaten—imprisoned by an illusionist's spirit that seemed to hang over the horizon of the dark, blue sky. The moonlight glowed brilliantly as each dream surrounded him in absolute silence.

There was a feeling of trouble unraveling his inner thoughts while the sun burned in the day's heat. The confusion seemed to reappear every sunrise at dawn and every sunset at dusk.

The warmth of the sunlight followed a chilly morning breeze. It appears the landscape had summoned the heat with lightning speed.

The heat surrounded him as gulps of hot air blew with no relief in sight. The heat seared him as he tried to keep his emotions and sanity intact. A feeling of doom grew.

There was no escaping the fierce struggle and sudden chase. In many ways, it was as if he were caged between the horror of the scorching desert and the garrison of Memphis.

The dust covered his sight momentarily as he pushed the horse to go faster. He didn't have a second to lose.

The sand irritated his eyes as the wind pushed dirt toward the sky. He glanced back, shading his eyes from the flying fragments, still moving as fast as he could.

The night descended into a sudden silence as the wind blew a swift breeze through the darkened African sky. There seemed to be no comfort during nighttime as he journeyed through the coldness and low humidity in darkness. His skin crawled as he fought the thick changing weather pattern of the desert.

In the dark of night, the misery increased. Aches and tearful eyes joined the weather intensity.

The desert was indeed to hide or run from demonic spirits. The demons were real, as if they were dancing in the blackest of nights. A lot of runaways had died there, the night carried a hideous growl. Moses had to learn to live a nomadic lifestyle.

Desert life was uncomfortable and seemed to torment his very soul. He was torn between desperation and what little strength the desire to survive gave him.

The desert was truly an uninhabitable wasteland, but it was a precious gift to escape through the rocky sand and crevices of the Earth to be isolated from view. He tried to calm his mind to focus in the right direction.

The chase seemed to form an endless wave that flowed across the desert sand. The image of death came full circle in the heat of summer. He attempted to avoid capture by moving swiftly away from the sounds of the galloping horses, but Smenkhare's forces were closing ranks. It was like a dream, but finally, his vision cleared. He stopped to catch his breath before moving on, realizing the enemy was gaining distance.

A cloud of dust swirled violently as the galloping horses roamed the desert. It was like a war had started in the middle of the desert.

His thoughts were twisted in anguish before fleeing in the heat. The madness was becoming an obsession as the troops moved closer and closer.

He made his way through the brush and the desert sand to escape the aggressors' ranks. He traveled as fast as his horse could carry him.

The bright light in the sky faded, brought the royal entourage into the presence of Smenkhare's forces in search of a fleeing prince.

There were shouts of warning and a growing threat of an internal struggle between two forces with the idea of loyalty between a divided Throne of Egypt. Frustration was swayed with a sudden panic that turned the capture into an intense confrontation between the two forces of Egypt, defying the king's orders.

The shouts got louder as acts of resistance in the rocky desert took place in the glowing sunlight while Smenkhare watched the prince from afar. The prince was in sight as the royal entourage closed in from the opposite direction. It was as if the prince had come to a dead end.

Shouts and sounds of galloping horses echoed, reaching Moses as he ran for safety from an act of treason. The time had come when the prince realized he was trapped like a wild animal.

He had no idea that the royal entourage was trying to help him. Daylight had fallen with the rays of sunlight getting stronger.

Smenkhare's forces straddled their horses, swaying in a circular motion and shifting their weight with an eagerness to attack the prince in the open landscape of the plain. Death was staring Moses straight in the face.

The sunlight seemed to leap between them as the soldiers waved their arms for courage, trying to catch up to Moses in the heat of the day. They were committed to fighting against Amarna as much as to fight against the prince.

One faction remained loyal to Memphis, intent on hunting down and killing Moses. In contrast, another group, devoted to Amarna, sought to protect the prince and ensure his safe passage to Ethiopia.

The guilt, anger, and frustration that once caused division and decreased Moses's chances of becoming Egypt's Pharaoh had dissipated significantly. Now, the only person in Egypt capable of granting freedom to the Israelites and releasing them from bondage was being pursued relentlessly like a wild animal.

Smenkhare's forces moved in orderly ranks, traveling on horseback and chariots under the protection of the pharaoh to capture or kill the prince.

Their grief was immense, driving them to consider attacking Nefertiti's forces and eliminating any obstacle in their path. Undeterred, they continued on their mission to capture the prince.

The nation was divided under two monarchs. One nation was under Amarna, and the other was loyal to Smenkhare, the banner of Memphis. The nation had become an unknown country.

Egypt was a country the prince loved, but his escape paved the way for a political movement that brought about protests how the nation treated its prisoners.

At a very young age, Moses established loyalty for Egypt and a bridge for the nation to heal from the dark path of injustice trifled by the fifth heavens. It seemed that the nation was bent on pretending that the demonic forces somehow wanted to bless them.

When Moses chose to break free from Egyptian customs, he faced rejection as their royal leader. He introduced his unique God and shared directions for his followers to serve the Hebrew faith.

The death of Akhenaten brought a division that not even the prince could heal. There was strife between Memphis and the city of Amarna because Akhenaten had built temples to worship Aten, the sun god.

The influence of the fifth heavens had become a powerful presence on the throne of Egypt, and the seventh heavens began to sow the seed of judgment in a nation that had turned away from their true source of blessings.

The curse of the seventh heavens would either force Egypt into submission or heighten the nation into civil unrest.

The mysterious power of the seventh heavens had taken away the power of the pagan gods in Egypt and touched the nation's soul most frighteningly.

The seventh heavens targeted women with children, the old, the young, and every animal. The Egyptians were on an unknown path of venom as cruel as the cold blizzard of winter.

There was no escaping the curse. The Egyptians abandoned their source of blessings and held on to falsehood with neither faith nor loyalty to their Creator.

The green, vast stretch of the mountainous gardens to the grasslands of the Sahara and the villages and towns along the Nile had been struck with a severe blow by the seventh heavens.

The flares had started to line up suddenly as though something imaginary was drawn into the nation's core. The situation in Egypt was becoming more complicated amid growing pain.

There were acts of wickedness raining down on the nation like an unseen cloud. The wind swayed night and day with a wild roar as panic filled the Egyptian territory.

The nation was divided by invisible forces and gripped with an unruly fate of justice. The glorious past had been snatched into a hopeless dream. It was like a constant nightmare with absolutely no possibility of moving forward. The land of plenty had been replaced with a curse!

The atmosphere shifted fast in the direction of chaos. Neither Aten nor Amun controlled political affairs in Egypt, but the nation struggled to keep its strength to survive.

The country itself was on the verge of insanity, with so little time left to survive. Yet even in this bitterness, the people still tried to hold on to their pagan gods. It was like the ticking of a clock. Nothing seemed to wake them from this creepy chaos. A sense of confusion was settling over the nation. It was a cruel blow from the seventh heavens.

The climate was becoming stranger and more unpredictable by the day. It seemed like something was haunting the nation.

There was fear of a long-lived nightmare troubling the people into mysterious drunkenness. The nation was beginning to transform into the image of death as if it had turned from one pagan god to another pagan god.

The dreams the pharaohs had for Egypt seemed to be turning into an illusion every day and night. The kind of future the pharaohs had imagined for the nation was a kind of blossoming prosperity, but something strange was in the air. The nation seemed to leap backward in time.

The mysterious power that once protected the nation had vanished. It was a fake covenant with the gods of the outer world! The pact with the pagan gods was trickery beyond the wild imagination.

The sun's rays became dim, and voices trembled at the throne in Amarna and Memphis in a frail weakness.

The crown of Egypt appeared to be in a fight between two forces of royal blood. The times had changed, and Moses's escape was a reminder of the new political climate in Egypt in the most extreme way.

The prince's escape marked a grim start for Egypt and sent shivers down Moses' spine as he endured the scorching and barren desert. Losing his royal powers after a privileged life as a prince left him feeling defenseless in the face of his new reality. His harsh living conditions served as constant reminders that his nobility had been stripped away. As a refugee, the price he paid was heavy, stirring up feelings of vengeance within him. Struggling with hunger and thirst, Moses faced a spiritual test that challenged his faith.

Every day was a new and different challenge to stay alive. He clung to his faith that his God would protect him in despair.

He was afraid. The pounding heartbeat never stopped. It was impossible to focus. His mind was too foggy with confusion.

He wanted to rest a little longer, but his hunger and concern for safety gave him no time to relax. He was fighting an intense, unbearable pain.

There was no simple answer, only a feeling of betrayal trapped within his inner soul. His mind had drifted senseless as though it would explode.

Moses' frustration grew as memories of Egypt conjured dark thoughts from his past – from childhood to his escape from the nation. What remained of his consciousness revisited the days spent worshiping alien deities. The mere idea sent shivers down his spine.

Despite once cherishing the land that nurtured his younger years, recollections now fueled his anger and exhaustion. As if reliving those moments only drew him closer to an unsettling realization. Clarity escaped him; only a sense of betrayal gnawed at his very core. His mind felt as if it would implode.

There was a stir of emotion as his memories made him understand that evil separated him from Egypt forever. The sub-tropical grassland and the galloping horses he learned to ride as a child remained in his mind. It didn't seem real that his haven had rejected him as a prince since he was an infant.

His eyes turned toward heaven in prayer and a renewed spirit. Each word was as bright as flames, filling his thoughts with unwavering faith. Somehow his thoughts were slowly crackling in the heat.

There was no escaping the memories from his youth that slipped around his life and separated him from the Israelites. The prince wanted to learn more about the behavior of the Israelites because it seemed the Egyptians never cared.

He knew the names of the priests and the military leaders, and he'd even served as an advisor to the king. The queen admired him and always managed to slip past the troublesome life the Israelites suffered daily.

Moses was convinced the endless pain his people endured had nothing to do with his life being a prince, but his interest in the matter was intense, and his hunger for fairness was long-lasting.

He was called a prince, while the Israelites became known as slaves to the pharaoh. He felt real guilt. It felt like an astonishing dream that might end at any moment.

Change swept Egypt, stirring political and religious reform that revolutionized the nation. The prince was caught up in a changing political climate that led to misery. He became an outcast from the country of his birth.

Night fell, and the temperature dropped sharply as the heat dissipated from the desert sand without any humidity to retain it.

His skin was tanned by the heat of the sun. The sun had darkened his skin to a reddish bronze color. He expected death at any moment, but his will to live wouldn't allow him to give up.

Hours drifted into days, and the sun's golden rays slowed his every move. It was a tough time, but he had enough energy to sustain his life. His thoughts plagued him, and pain clung to him like a cloud.

There were endless sleepless nights that curbed his desire to move forward. A glance over his shoulder suddenly brought into view troops gaining distance between them.

He stared into the blue African sky and hurried ahead of the advancing cavalry. Closer and closer, the cavalry moved toward the prince through the strain of darkness.

For a moment, the overflowing darkness saved the prince from the fury of Smenkhare.

When night fell, they slowed, shifting the chase in the prince's favor. The cavalry was too tired to care now. Tiredness and drowsiness forced the cavalry to pause the hunt.

The cavalry was drunk with fatigue. They were exhausted and wanted to rest.

The desert was like an inferno in daylight and cold during nightfall. Those who had fallen victim to the chase were scorched by the sun's heat and eaten by scavengers.

Moses felt the emotions of being unsanitary and the smell of human flesh. The thought of foulness in his clothes and wild men chasing him day and night kept him on edge.

That awful feeling of being outnumbered in unfamiliar terrain drove him to a sudden madness. His heartbeat raced with emotion, and unspeakable panic ran wildly through his mind.

There was so much emotion that Smenkhare could almost taste victory with the capture so nearby. Smenkhare and his troops continued with an intense thirst for blood in the pitch dark.

The prince maneuvered past the danger, leading the troops on a long chase through the rocky desert sand.

The night turned into day, and the sun shone with radiant rays of light like an enormity of current from the uttermost of the sky.

A feeling of exhaustion appeared in his dark brown eyes, and a look of fatigue clouded his face. He could feel his flesh burning from the fiery heat as he moved swiftly through the dry air.

Almost in a daze of confusion, he heard the galloping horses with the troops at his rear. He knew the troops were gaining ground.

The sudden progression of the troops turned into a swift chase. The prince was determined to get away but could not increase his speed anymore as he stared straight ahead.

The enemies were near, and time seemed to halt with his fiercest foe appearing at a striking distance. He had no thought of giving up, but the thread of fear was trapped in his imagination while traveling through branches, barely able to focus at the edge of his vision.

The troops were on the verge of capturing Moses in the stifling heat when the royal entourage, the prince's faithful protector, approached the cavalry in a fierce standoff. They moved closer to the troops. It was a step closer to an all-out war.

They circled Smenkhare's troops, virtually encasing them within their ranks with a flare of rage.

They swayed in a circle, shifting their horses around and around while encasing Smenkhare's forces and yelling insults and swearing as the heat of friction intensified. The wild rage of vengeance flowed like a stream of boiling blood.

A vibrance of energy and a rush of fresh blood ran through his veins as other defenses of the royal entourage surrounded the prince. His heart constricted into a panic before he recognized the royal escort was there for his protection.

The prince was breathless, but there was a surge of hope that he'd live another day.

Perhaps his mind drifted with excitement as confusion clouded his mind. He took a deep breath as fear gave way to bravery, as his face revealed his surprise. The dark side engulfed his every thought. He wasn't sure what was happening as he embraced the unusual moment with a deep breath.

The prince felt the brilliance of life again. A sudden vision and sensation of shock made him unaware of what might be the outcome of his fate.

The stir of emotions siphoned fear away with each heartbeat that grew with a burst of fresh energy.

He gasped for air as the sweet sting of safety pounded like an excited pulse of liveliness. He tried to catch his breath as the blood rushed through his body. A look of defiance appeared on his face with what little strength he had left.

The prince didn't say anything at all. He just sat there on his horse and listened. He had no idea what to expect.

Despite the fear, the prince never felt disloyal or guilty for defending an Israelite in the heat of the moment.

He was still alive as the noise echoed around him again and again. In a way, he still had the strength of a prince. No matter his past mistakes, he was protected by the royal entourage.

In the engagement, there were more shouts than physical fighting. The cavalry certainly felt threatened by those loyal to Nefertiti, and Smenkhare considered the reaction nothing short of treason.

The soldiers were orderly until chaos from the heated exchange descended into disarray.

That very day the sun's rays burned bright with feverish heat. It was too hot for any interference from the royal entourage.

There was a blaze of tension across the eastern sky as insults spewed into the dry air. Without wasting a minute, the king asked for the prince's surrender. They wanted his head on a stake!

The troops loyal to Smenkhare became entangled with a desire to shatter the dreams and vision of the prince with brutal force. They stumbled about, shouting and turning mindlessly to the loud sounds of galloping horses.

The king's eyes were fixed on Prince Moses as though the thought of escape was forbidden. The chase had come to an end. There was nothing the prince could do.

All eyes were fixed on the prince. There was an awkward moment as frustration and sweat from the chase soaked their bodies.

Within moments, the imperial war machine of Egypt ceased to be the most feared army on the battlefield. There was nothing to unite them! They were divided by supernatural entities that changed the fate of the nation.

The two imperfect forces of Memphis and Amarna separated Egypt to the point of no return. The division was a trapped and laid out by the fifth heavens.

Still, some soldiers were caught up in a vicious confusion. In the mind of Smenkhare, this was the greatest form of betrayal. Moses stayed on his horse while the entourage encircled him.

Whispers surrounded him as they waited. One soldier bowed and said, "We have come to escort you to safety, Prince Moses."

Deep inside his thoughts, Moses felt reprieve when he'd learned an entourage of Ethiopian troops had come to escort him safely to the African nation.

The passing of time didn't cure anything. Smenkhare and his cavalry were still full of madness. The king sat silently as he swelled with anger. The prince's escape to freedom was too much for him to bear.

After all, the king wanted revenge even though Nefertiti's forces and the Ethiopian brigade outnumbered them. The king wouldn't be satisfied until Prince Moses was dead.

There was fresh hope and a small burst of happiness as things unfolded in the prince's favor. A load had been lifted off his shoulders. His heart was still racing in a bit of shock.

There was no way Smenkhare would allow the former prince to strive for freedom so quickly. His ego wouldn't allow the king to forgive Moses.

That phase of Egyptian life passed, and he was overcome by a sense of alienation and hostility from Smenkhare's forces.

He could feel the anger in the scornful glares as the prince slipped away. He was still unsure how he'd be received in Ethiopia.

A loose cry flowed from the king's throat for the troops to charge forward. The king was unhinged and not a moment too soon. His face was muddy and without a doubt of fear.

Some of Smenkhare's forces advanced through the dusty haze, attempting to capture the prince. He couldn't wait another moment. With a silent command and arms waving for balance, cries of vengeance filled the desert air.

Meanwhile, other soldiers became engaged in the intense battle. Anyone who ventured out to kill Moses was too absorbed in the chaos to consider the consequences.

Blood flowed on the battlefield, and the chanting gave the cavalry the confidence to carry out their mission to capture or kill the prince.

Some roars rang out with shouts, and crackling of fiery arcs from hot metal in the air. The chaos of hatred and fighting filled the morning air. Like a spoiled child, the king had no shame and indulge in the shameful humiliation of his hostility toward the prince.

Suddenly, Smenkhare dashed forward with a hideous yell before being struck down by an Ethiopian sword. His body dangled in midair as the sand from the galloping horses flew up, showering the king as his silhouette fell wildly to the ground.

The nation's fate instantly became as divided as day and night. Smenkhare's lifeless body lay covered in dirt as his soldiers paused briefly in shock. The vision of revenge was gone!

In the heat of the battle, some tried to run away from the swiftness of the Ethiopian troops but could find no escape route. Others fell to their knees to surrender to the royal entourage. No matter how horrifying the battle became, the royal entourage stood on the sidelines and allowed Smenkhare's forces to be slaughtered.

CHAPTER 14

HOREMHEB AND HIS WARRIORS returned to Amarna, while Prince Moses escaped living his life in an Ethiopia province. Perhaps his one God, Yahweh, was protecting him the whole time.

After all, Moses rejected Atenism and, for a long time, was respected by the powerful ruling class of Egypt. Prince Moses was wise and bold enough to show his love for the oppressed Israelites and the ordinary citizens in Egypt.

The city of Amarna was now back in charge of Egyptian affairs, and they were unified under one monarch, regardless of the pain of losing the co-ruler and the beloved prince. Nefertiti was now in charge with full pharaonic authority, but a deadly epidemic was raging across the empire, again putting the nation's fate in question.

Egypt was still trapped by malicious forces as if time had reached out to bind it with a vital blow. The queen was among the first victims of the sudden illness that spread across the Empire. Before any celebration of victory, Nefertiti was stricken by a fever and pneumonia and died.

Lightening flashed across the African sky with an intense friction in the dry air. The sky glowed with a furious display, radiating through the air with thunder.

There was a struggle for power between Meritaten, the eldest daughter of Nefertiti, and Kiya, the minor wife of Akhenaten.

The influence of Kiya continued to grow in Nefertiti's absence. Yet, the real power resided with the chief minister, Saga Ay, the grandfather of Meritaten, who swore his granddaughter, the chosen successor.

When Akhenaten was alive, Meritaten was called Mayati, meaning "the mistress of your house." Meritaten had Kiya evicted from the Maru Temple at South Amarna and moved her into the harem palace.

Kiya was outraged. Her thoughts became filled with venom. Her grip on power loosened as she was removed from political affairs.

Throughout the dark nights of Egypt, a deadly epidemic ravaged the land, leaving fear and devastation in its path. The first wave struck with blinding lightning and deafening thunder, terrorizing the city of Memphis daily. Egypt's revered and powerful gods had abandoned the nation, vanishing at the first sign of the ominous events from the seventh heavens.

The Egyptians were fighting a nightmare threatening to turn the nation into another disaster. The nation was crushed between two unseen powers. Confusion was meant to lead them onto a certain path.

The religious system the Egyptians trusted for their safety had diminished with abnormal floods. The rubble from the floods polluted the lush fields of the Nile River Valley. Their sacred land was no longer stable or blessed as an earthly paradise.

To the Egyptians, the water from the Nile River was considered sacred and a gift from the gods. The beginning of the plagues brought large quantities of red dirt down from the highland of Ethiopia. This carried disease-infested fish and gave the river an appearance of blood.

A rotten stench arose from the Nile, causing the nearby spring water to become as bitter and unpalatable as the river itself. Hapi, the god in charge of the annual flood and protector of fish, was powerless. This shift in climate transformed the Nile's abundance into a problem. The weather took a rapid turn, signaling that the gods of the outer realms were on a destructive spree.

There were Indra and Montu, falcon gods of war, and Hathor, the famine god of love. Thot, often depicted as a man with a sacred ibis-headed animal or baboon, was god of wisdom. Osiris was characterized by the mythical Bennu bird, and was seen as the god of death and the afterlife. In Egypt, Maat was depicted as a woman with an ostrich feather on her head and goddess of truth and justice.

There was a god for everything in Egypt. They were brought through myths and legends from the Greeks living in Egypt, but they all disappeared during distress.

Amun-Ra, Aten, and all the rest of the forces of the fifth heavens became absent during the time of trouble.

Akhenaten began his reign promoting his one and only god, Aten, the divine rays of the sun disc. He revolutionized religion and culture and created a high standard of artistic and architectural achievements.

In the royal thoughts of the king, Aten stood above all other Egyptian deities. The whole empire found itself engulfed in a fierce battle for power, leading to its downfall. The idea of their gods abandoning them was beyond imagination. Chaos emerged, with the land consumed by an eerie, unnatural disturbance.

Akhenaten was gone, and the throne was threatened with divisiveness. At the end of Akhenaten's life, his mind became exhausted with guilt and shameful tears of rejection, which wouldn't allow him to rest day or night.

Even Aten disappeared, leaving the mighty imperial war machine in shambles. The Egyptians rejected their source of blessings, given by the God of the Hebrews, and chose to worship the polytheistic gods of their enslavers.

The plagues brought disgrace upon the polytheistic gods, who the Egyptians served with a degree of respect.

The lethal epidemic rapidly spread through the population. It seemed as though the ancient gods from distant realms sought to taunt the nation with an act of retribution. These otherworldly deities had never harbored any affection for Egypt.

The polluted water led the city to stink of dead fish and foul odor, and the river changed between green, blue, and red.

The blessings of the Nile supplied abundant wealth, including varieties of fish and valuable salts, water for irrigating plants and drinking water for human and animal consumption.

The obnoxious stink of death and growing misery from an insufficient supply of meat and drinking water still wasn't enough to reject these polytheistic gods. The seventh heavens were also on a war path until the Egyptians cast away polytheism.

The sun was covered by a thick, dark cloud, which loomed over the nation like a magical spell.

The red-bearded god of thunder and rain was angry and brought misery at the sight of the Egyptians turning away.

Their low whispering voice appeared to exercise faith in the old gods of the nation. It was a terrible time in the Egyptian Empire devoid of peace and brimming with insidious filth.

As the river cast out the dead from the sea, the sun god and other polytheistic gods allowed the Egyptians to suffer the fate of starvation—and slow miserable demise.

Different variations of religious sects worshipped the polytheistic faith of the outer world of the fifth heavens.

The nation continued to transform into a hideous concept of evil. The power of the outer world continued to exist in the nation's mind with a passion for various gods. Emotions were growing as the mysterious shadow of death turned the nation into darkness.

There was still admiration and some uncertainty for the fifth heavens. Maybe it was an illusion haunting the nation like a dim light drifting into darkness.

Death was everywhere. The light that once illuminated Egypt was now dim. The hymns that echoed across the empire came to an intense silence.

The stillness of the fifth heavens succeeded, with no escaping the vengeance from the dawn of morning deep into the night. The nation slipped into a strange and unimaginable place during the Amarna era.

The Amarna period roughly lasted for twenty years, but the impact embraced the misery of death and malice for those who failed to convert to Atenism. Even Meritaten, the Great Royal Wife, was short-lived with no male heir. Her name meant "She who is beloved of Aten."

Before Meritaten could make amends with Amun-Ra, she fell sick less than two years after becoming royal queen. The damage was done, and the beloved queen was dead.

The gods Akhenaten banned were blamed for all the destruction happening throughout Egypt. The fear of death was poisoning the air. Kiya, the second wife of Akhenaten, never spoke of becoming queen of the nation again. There was an intense silence on her lips.

The fear was confirmed. Her life was filled with doubt, which she often felt during her marriage to Akhenaten. Her insecurity was fueled by never becoming royal queen and remaining second to Nefertiti.

Kiya's exact function was unclear. The only known authority she possessed remained at the harem palace. Her low whispering voice blended into the shadows.

She wanted to avoid any curse, like the plague that was sweeping across Egypt, and weakening the nation after each wave. Aten, the god of love, peace, and joy, fled, and his shining rays seemed to disappear into oblivion.

The light of Aten no longer encircled Egypt for the nation's protection. The faith of Aten became unbearable. It was bitter, as if there was little respect for the god of the sun disc.

That gleam of hope Akhenaten had trusted for so long tore the nation apart and trampled Egypt into an awkward silence. In times of trouble, Aten became a bizarre fable with empty promises.

This marked the end of an era, but the Egyptians chose to believe the old gods of Egypt were angry with the nation.

There was no escaping the misery of death, and dark energy was haunting the nation like a bad dream. Panic was sweeping through the air as far as the eye could see.

CHAPTER 15

The plague shifted the nation's religious culture, but there was no sickness for the Israelites. The Israelites were spared from that misery and became energized with the desire for freedom.

A miraculous blessing awakened the souls of those who had faith in the sovereign God of the Hebrew people. The gods of the Egyptians were as cunning as the religious leaders who wanted to acquire as much wealth as possible. Their fate rested in the one God, Yahweh.

It'd been twenty years since Raphael arrived in Egypt, but his prophecy rang out like flames of fire: "By this, you shall know that I am the Lord: behold, I will strike the water that is in the Nile with the staff that is in my hand, and it will be turned to blood. The fish in the Nile will die, and the Nile will become foul, and the Egyptians will find difficulty in drinking water from the Nile."

The people grew afraid of the plague that had come upon the nation, and fear seemed to leap into the hearts of the elites and ordinary citizens. The royal court would be the first administration to flee from Amarna.

The nine-year-old king, Tutankhaten, and his queen, Ankhsenamun, moved the royal residence back to Memphis and abandoned Amarna, the home of his father, Akhenaten.

Tutankhaten issued a decree restoring the sanctuaries, idol worship, personnels, and priesthood privileges to venerate the old gods. Again, Amun became the chief god of the nation.

His most trusted advisors, General Horemheb and Grand Vizier Ay, became very concerned over the political weakness and turmoil that had plagued the nation since they'd abandoned their polytheistic gods.

King Tut was a traitor! The king eventually abandoned Aten, the reaching rays of the sun. It was as if some wild spirit of the unknown devoured him. The moment had come and gone in the faith of Aten, the sun disc. He wanted to serve Amun and share his faith far away from Amarna.

There was a gentle breeze and a taste of freedom that miraculously struck the nation. A splash of liberty filled the air.

A cool breeze drifted across the nation, with traces of sunlight penetrating the darkness.

The people began to serve the gods of their choice, especially the elders who remembered the nation's past glory. Despite the warm breeze of freedom, a dark cloud of division was still hovering over the nation.

Under the leadership of King Tut, his advisors sought to restore the sanctuaries of the old gods and goddesses. He changed his name from Tutankhaten to Tutankhamun, meaning "Living image of Amun," restoring the cult of Amun.

King Tutankhamun reversed the role of Aten, lifted the ban against the god of Amun, and restored the traditional privileges of the priesthood.

Tutankhamun dropped the radical changes of embracing Aten and returned Thebes to the local priesthood in favor of Amun. Laborers that built the temples, administration districts, and the new canal drainages were all out of work. The priests of Aten, artistic decorators, and foreign and domestic workers had to find work elsewhere.

The divine rays of Aten, the sun disc, lost their heat, bringing misery and degradation in civil and religious services. The new, young king abandoned the city of Amarna, but other administrative roles remained there.

There was no looking back. People were dying throughout the empire, and the reaching rays of Aten were blamed for the devastation. A darkness passed over the east side of the royal temple, striking the Nile's water with the appearance of blood. The celestial forces were moving across the landscape of the empire with a sudden rage.

A dark cloud covered the sun, and the bystander's eyes seemed glued to the sky. Their eyes were widening with fear. They were bewildered and stunned breathless.

Even the water stored in vessels and wood barrels became bitter and undrinkable. There was nothing there but fear.

In the cities, there was no hope. The absence of sanitation left the nation in a twisted faith of uncertainty, and a reign of terror struck the nation in her darkest days. The nation was in a daze and a gush of confusion.

The sun was sinking in the twilight of darkness. Thunder and lightning crackled through the atmosphere like a bad dream. The fiery sky burst open with heavy raindrops as if every storm was a warning from the heavens.

The Pharaoh's most trusted magicians gave the water the appearance of blood through the power of the fifth heavens. There was a certain amount of confusion with enchantment in effort to display fiery influences of light from the outer world. The lying wonders displayed incredible powers briefly, while Sekhmet, the goddess of devastation, attempted to imitate the God of the Hebrew people.

The Hebrew religion and Atenism embraced a monotheistic god without a statue or graven image. Now, these magicians had made the water appear red as blood.

Then suddenly, the gods of the fifth heavens fled. There was an intense silence. The powers of the magicians vanished like a lifeless nightmare. The angels of the seventh heavens came forth in majestic and towered over the nation of Egypt. The angelic order of the seventh heavens did not come for peace but to create devastation for the unbelievers.

The absence of the fifth heavens left the illusionists with nothing but fear. The fear spread like wildfire as every day brought a different horror.

Raphael had prophetic visions and wrestled with his dreams. His visions featured a series of plagues and horrible deaths that rested upon the people of Egypt. While others returned to the old gods of Egypt, some shifted their belief to the God of the Israelites.

The Creator God was not only the supreme deity of the Israelites but also the architect of the entire universe, responsible for crafting both the spiritual and physical realms, including the sky, Earth, and seas.

The one true God created the forces of nature, with the power of the universe at His disposal to use as He desires. The Creator God was even willing to offer salvation to the Egyptians.

The grand vizier immediately defined the converts as treacherous and treated conversion to the Hebrew faith with the same oppression as the Israelites living in Egypt. They were looked upon as traitors, and those who decided to praise the monolithic God of the Hebrew faith were threatened with death.

When Raphael closed his eyes, a vision from the heavens seemed to fill his thoughts. The dream was an escape from reality and the stillness that had entangled him since his arrival to work in the royal palace of the pharaoh. The sun had turned his skin a deeper and darker bronze from toiling long hours in the heat.

Once more, his dreams had rescued him from the bitter truth of being a slave of the vizier. The dreams became more mystified with every gleaming thought. A feeling of damnation grew. There was no escaping the grief and sudden nightmares.

The young Egyptian ruler, King Tut, relied heavily on his General of the Army, Horemheb, and Grand Vizier, Ay - the chief minister of Egypt - to govern the nation. As the plague increasingly impacted Egypt's economy, the government became more dependent on the Israelites for the country's advancement.

Differently, the forces of nature made growing food more difficult, and workers continued to build irrigation channels. New farming techniques rested with the Israelites living under oppression. The prophecy continued: "Let my people go so they may worship Me. If you refuse to let them, go, I will send a plague of frogs to your country. The Nile will teem with frogs. They will come up into your palace and your bedroom and onto your bed, into the houses of your officials and your people, and your ovens and kneading troughs. The frogs will come up on you, your people, and all your officials."

Even during the night, the terrible signs of the plague didn't allow them to escape the horror. There was no defense. The epidemic struck the nation suddenly. Life was being drained out of the empire.

The arsenal of confusion struck like a flash of lightning as if it was a sort of horror speaking through the force of nature. There were sleepless nights, and many were desperate and hungry. No one was spared from the horror.

The pain became deeper. The nation was lost in darkness like a wicked curse roaming so delicately. The river was polluted, and frogs began to leap out of the water. The whistling sound of wind and thunder came chirping like guided bombs.

The awfulness of nature had become fearful. A mixture of blood from dead carcasses and red mud was brought down from the Ethiopian Highland. The life-giving river of the Nile had become worthless. The water was flowing with the appearance of blood.

Foreign gods invaded the sacred river of the Nile, and the Egyptians became partakers in human sacrifice by casting little children into the river as sacrificial offerings to calm Hapi, the god of the Nile.

The children of the Israelites had become victims of this cruel ritual to appease the gods of the outer world.

The cries of helpless children became a habitual sin to please the gods brought down from the Balkans, who wanted to separate the Egyptians from the Israelites.

There was a notion of appeasing the gods of the outer world with the sacrifice of blood to quench the thirst of the fifth heavens. The calm never came. Only panic and great sorrow deepened throughout the nation.

The nation was on different courses and trapped in the torment of two spiritual powers.

Thunder rumbled in the sky with a surge of lightning overhead as flashes split the sky from night to daylight. Fear was clinging to the nation like a cruel nightmare.

The God of Judgment was angry and sent messengers to urge a transformation to abandon the gods of the fifth heavens. The gods of the fifth heavens wouldn't dare to interfere. The pain worsened as a thick fog settled on the bank of the river. A breeze of confusion made the nation tremble with anguish and fear.

In each gentle breeze, a foul odor polluted the air and sent swarms of frogs into the depth of the cities. The smell carried by the wind, rain, and heat from the sun intensified the polluted river of the Nile.

CHAPTER 16

OVER THE NEXT FORTY YEARS, Moses lived a pastoral life in Midian. Back in Egypt, the Israelites continued to multiply exceedingly despite cruelty from the pharaoh.

The plague carried a flash of panic large enough to change the pharaoh's mind. The terror swept the Nile, bringing more labor and pain from building large projects around the empire.

There came a moment when the heavens were shut up, and young men dug around the rivers to find clean drinking water, but all they found was a spring of blood.

The drought made them wonder if, somehow, they'd angered the gods of the outer world and become cursed with the absence of rain.

The heavens broke loose, sending hail, fire, and thunder down upon the Egyptian farmland. Flashes of fire rolled down from the sky, with clouds lingering over the horizon. The fireballs of lightning and echoing thunder entered the skyline, wave after wave as if they were pursuing vengeance.

The hail came, falling on all the crops and shattering every tree in the fields. The frightening storm gushed over animal shelters and houses as the shepherds panicked.

Through Moses, the Israelites learned of their covenant with the Creator God. The God of the Israelites would renew the Covenant, leading them out of exile into a brighter future—if they served their monotheistic Creator.

They were brought the knowledge of a savior, the God of Israel, but the two groups of angels in the heavens continued to be at war.

The plague brought a tighter yoke on the Israelites and started a cause to move the administration buildings away from the epidemic.

The land of Goshen was the original dwelling that the Israelites had settled while Grand Vizier Joseph was alive. The city of Goshen became an administrative district and living quarters to get away from the plague.

The Israelites were tasked with reconstructing the ancient capital city of the Hyksos along the northeastern Nile Delta. However, rest was unattainable as the plague spread rapidly, causing immense chaos and confusion.

Every non-disabled person had to join to provide labor. The Israelites were expected to perform long periods of work and complete tasks like erecting monuments and massive cave carving projects in the mountains.

The rules were strictly enforced, and fear grew in the minds of the Egyptians trying to survive the natural occurrence brought down the Nile by the plague.

Within the town, the persistent clamor of frogs led residents to believe that the end was nowhere in sight. The air was thick with frustrated cries.

Moses took his flock to graze in the mountains called Sinai. Mount Sinai was nearly untouchable. It was grassland at the highest peak of the mountains where other shepherds dared not travel for fear of God, who was rumored to dwell there. It was the perfect place to talk to the Creator.

He drove his flock to the highest point on Mount Sinai, which provided the best pasture grazing. Here is where a fire uttered a voice from a burning bush.

That day changed Prince Moses from a simple shepherd to a courageous prophet sent to rescue the Israelites from bondage. The burning bush was engulfed with an eternal flame that had the power of God.

It took a moment for Moses to process the flames from the burning bush. Moses turned aside and saw this incredible sight, why the bush is not consumed. A voice called out of the burning, paving the way for the divine encounter. Moses listened to the voice and the concern to lead the Israelites to freedom.

The bush burned like a continuous flame when Moses asked, "When I come unto the children of Israel and shall say unto them, 'The God of your fathers hath sent me unto you; and they shall say unto me, 'what is his name?'"

Then God said unto Moses, "I am that I am: Thus, shalt thou say unto the children of Israel, 'He who is hath sent me unto you.'" The voice from the burning bush continued, "Go to the king and tell hm that the Lord says, 'Let my people go so that they can worship me. If you refuse, I will punish your country by covering it with frogs.'"

Moses returned to Egypt on a divine mission to convince King Tut or the grand vizier to let the people go. He tried to persuade the king to allow the Israelites to escape bondage and so they can praise their God in their promised land of Israel.

The messengers that came before Moses had no success in convincing the king that the great pains of the nation were due to the bondage of the Israelites.

Ay was the boy king's grand vizier, his royal chancellor who had gained the respect of ordinary people, priests, and the pharaoh. The grand vizier had no intention of allowing the Israelites to leave Egypt for fear of losing profit from their labor.

Recently, the young King Tut took charge of a government that cherished liberty and freedom. Grand Vizier Ay rose to prominence, becoming Egypt's most powerful figure and serving as the royal chancellor. Despite his youth, the king retained his divine status. As the royal chancellor, Ay took control of most government services, answering only to King Tut himself.

The divine status of the pharaoh added to the hostility when the croaking of the frogs spread across the nation and became a tremendous discomfort. The pharaoh had no power to reduce the multitude of frogs, and his magicians only increased the plague when they attempted to replicate the curse brought on by the Nile.

The magicians wanted to prove to the grand vizier that they could duplicate the power of the Hebrew God, but they only brought misery to the land of Egypt.

For a moment, the false prophets and magicians considered that the swarms of frogs they produced were a miracle, but soon their arrogance against the Hebrew God faded. The people rose, calling the false prophets demonic and ministers of evil.

The messengers informed the grand vizier that what Egypt was experiencing came through the will of the One God of the Hebrew people.

However, the boy king and grand vizier Ay were in disbelief and called their words a deceitful trick. They claimed their priests and magicians could also do the magical arts.

Prince Moses cast his rod upon the ground to prove the power was from a superior God much more divine than the priests, magicians, or any gods from the fifth heavens and commanded the rod to turn into a serpent.

It obeyed, turning itself into a serpent like a dragon. The serpent devoured the rods of the Egyptians. Again, the serpent turned itself back into the form of a rod while the prince held it in his hand.

However, the boy king became angry, believing this mysterious endeavor was no more than trickery and a cunning way to relieve the Israelites from daily labor. The king said that they would gain nothing from this shrewdness.

The grand vizier ordered that the Israelites maintain their tasks of manual brickmaking and processing grain for livestock.

The boy king despised Moses and threatened the prince with enslavement, but the river continued to run with bloody water not fit to drink. Whether in Amarna or Thebes, the children of Israel continued to experience hard labor and felt moments of darkness and increased lashes.

In Amarna, the city continued to burn bright from the sun's rays, but in some ways, they were still terrified of the unknown, which seemed to change every day and night.

The country had evolved into something unrecognizable, leaving its citizens aware of an avenging deity in an alarming manner. The ancient capital's magnificent temples required reconstruction. The people revered the sun as the ultimate creator, and this belief thrived vibrantly in Amarna, the city dedicated to the sun god, Aten.

In their daily lives, the Israelites witnessed the idolatry of sun worshippers in the old and new capital cities. Their trust remained in the pagan gods of the outer world to bring an end to this severe famine.

A number of Israelites joyfully took part in these ceremonies, expressing their deep gratitude towards the fifth heavens and the Egyptians alike for rescuing them from the devastating plagues that struck the Nile.

Egypt's golden days swiftly faded with every moment due to the calamity of frogs consuming the crops. There were also dead animals everywhere.

The country was full of slime from the frogs roaming through living quarters and turning homes into disease-infested accommodations. The smell of decay and destruction hovered as the wind blew a distasteful aroma into the air.

Moses tried to persuade the king to allow the Israelites a safe journey to Mount Sinai, so they could worship their God and remove the plague, but the king had no regard for the words of Moses and mocked him.

Moses went back to Egypt, not as a beloved prince but as a prophet of their one God, declaring unto the Israelites that the Creator "hath sent me unto you."

"He is not Aten nor Amun-Ra, but a God that will serve you day and night," said Moses.

The boy king responded, "Let the Israelites worship which ever god pleases them as long as they complete their tasks."

The children of Israel weren't persuaded by Moses, having been alienated from the God of their fathers for such a long time. They were oppressed by the same nation that once provided them with haven.

The king had no regard for the words that Moses spoke, and he trusted the gods of Egypt to loosen their grip upon the nation. To the Egyptians, the frog was a symbol of the goddess, Heqt, who represented fertility and was related to the annual flooding of the Nile.

The river gave life to the fertile region of the Nile and was associated with women during childbirth. The polluted water from the Nile forced the frogs out of the river with an ungrateful smell. This changed the natural protocol from life to death by a superior power much greater than the goddess, Heqt.

Through a strange twist of fate, the king ordered Moses to take the Israelites and be gone. The king granted them liberty out of fear but not from the fullness of his heart. The moment the Israelites were freed, he withdrew his decision. His gut clenched as the Israelites journeyed away from their oppression.

Observing his former captives stride confidently away from Egypt, his heart suddenly hardened due to an inexplicable frenzy, was a feat of mental fortitude.

There was a brief chill when the frogs vanished, and an awareness of normalcy caused the king to change his mind. The river cleared, and the land returned to its former nature.

His eyes rolled instantly as a sudden rage traveled through his veins. He ordered the Israelites to turn back. Moses could only watch while the Israelites went back into bondage to suffer their fate.

Suddenly, the Nile Delta erupted in a volcanic explosion that sent a cloud of ash and tidal waves down the coast of the Nile. The fall out rode the waves and polluted the river, shifting everyone into a mood for survival.

The cataclysmic event unearthed creepy insects that were buried beneath the ground. Everywhere there was death.

Countless flies, vast numbers of lice, and voracious insects emerged from the ground's opening. The sheer mass of these creatures transformed daylight into an eerie darkness, as if night had suddenly enveloped the world.

Devastation and the depth of darkness brought a specific black smoke along the Nile, and the air seemed to suck the life out of the nation. Fragments of Earth bombarded the region, and contaminated hot air depopulated the coastline. Some were dying slowly as the black fume of smoke filled their lungs. The result was disastrous!

Egypt's decline began when invaders from the Balkans arrived, introducing a new and enigmatic culture. Driven by envy, they acted against the Israelites, tightening their grip on the once-peaceful nation. This foreign presence ignited animosity within Egyptian society. The government's view of the Israelites shifted from warm hospitality to undeserved contempt, likely influenced by their own experiences of suffering and subjugation.

Both Egyptians and Israelites found themselves shackled by the dominating Balkan presence. National pride soon replaced the once-esteemed status of Israeli citizens, and the burdensome chains of oppression were not far behind.

The Balkan invaders spread a form of bigotry that separated the Egyptians from the Israelites. The invaders destroyed the Egyptians' respect for the Israelites on the highest level.

The events that unfolded inflicted pain, sparking a divide among the African people that rippled across Mesopotamia. In the process, the spiritual essence that once graced the Egyptians vanished during the time of the Greek invaders.

These intruders exploited cultural disparities to separate Mediterranean communities. This rift, initiated by the fifth heavens, turned the Israelites' privileged status into a life of servitude.

As the Europeans arrived, they introduced a fresh set of dynamic rules that transformed the nation, allowed physical aggression in exchange for economic growth, and shared their inherent convictions. The Egyptians' Golden Age met its end due to disasters unleashed from the seventh heavens, serving as retribution for Egypt's transgressions against the Israelites.

Madness was vigorously stirred in Egypt as if the fifth heavens had crept in at the dawn of darkness and snatched the soul out of the nation.

Raphael warned the priests to reject every kind of graven image or idol worship, and the Creator strictly forbade the veneration of the stars.

After all, the sight of death became a standard concept, among other things haunting Egypt. The new monarch initiated a religious revolution away from Aten toward the old Amun faith, abandoning his father's cult.

The worship of the outer world's celestial spheres of the fifth heavens was only a trap.

As the plague rose throughout the Nile Delta, gleams of extreme heat, floods, dangerous wind, and lightning entered the horizon beneath the dark, blue sky. Many were forced to drink the unhealthy water coming from the Nile. Drinking the water caused diseases to spread throughout the cities.

More and more people died from the wrath, so much that the water brought pain and a bitter torment upon the land of Egypt. The mysterious plague brought death and sickness across the grand land-scape of Egypt and changed the nation's fabric.

People were dying throughout Egypt. The public and animals struggled to survive the awful climate beneath the darkened sky. The plague brought about distaste for the cult of Aten, and it became weaponry for Moses, who the pharaoh blamed for the destructive atmosphere. This deadly epidemic was bringing havoc upon Egypt in the worst possible way.

The religious cult of Amun and the faith of Egypt's elite class arose from the ashes and replaced the official state cult of Aten, the reaching rays of the sun god.

The effect of the plague nourished a red toxin that turned the Nile into a bloodlike color. The water supply had to be purified, and filtering became a daily life. The acidic ash reached livestock and brought more famine. Cattle perished, carrying contaminated sores, and boiling at an alarming rate.

There was no answer to the plagues, but the pharaoh didn't yield. Instead, he threatened to cut off Moses's head if he brought more trouble to Egypt.

Moses stretched his hand toward the sky, and darkness covered the nation. The sun became dull, and the light rays refused to illuminate the gloomy sky.

A gray cloud settled over the horizon, and darkness blocked the sun for three days. The darkened clouds descended over the nation with thunderbolts of lightning amid a mighty hailstorm.

In broad daylight, the rays of sunlight were blotted out and hidden from the African sky. The path was paved for the gods of the outer world to descend upon the nation like a fierce cloud in the dark of night.

It was a wild and strange scene when daylight plunged into darkness, and the sea broke with the sounds of thunder. A terrible storm carrying huge waves covered the land. The waves soared into cabins, and vessels sailing violently down the Nile were at the mercy of the surge.

Ships were tossed around at the height of the storm as the rain and hail came down. Strikes of fire mysteriously burst out of the night sky and touched the roughness of the sea.

The sound of wind rumbled through the darkness and broke trees into pieces. After the hail ceased, swarms of locusts wiped out any vegetation that had survived the hailstorm.

The insects reproduced at an alarming rate, impeding the work cycle. The harder they worked, the more the insects intensified and stung—even during nighttime.

Many crops were yet to be planted, but the locusts and grasshoppers consumed the seeds. Yet, there was no hail in the land of Goshen, where the Israelites lived.

The severe storm brought so much terror that the Egyptians repented for mistreating the Israelites and began weeping heavy tears. The Egyptians cried out for forgiveness, but the pharaoh was too afraid to abandon his most beloved god, Amun-Ra.

The young pharaoh confessed his sins to the heavens and asked Moses to pray for him, saying, "Go worship the Lord. Even your women and children may go with you; only leave your flocks and herds behind." The pharaoh had been persuaded to allow the Israelites to leave, and he told Moses to take his people out of Egypt.

However, Moses said, "You must allow us to have sacrifices and burn offerings to present to the Lord, our God. Our livestock, too, must go with us; not a hoof is to be left behind."

To the astonishment of Pharaoh, the swarm of locusts and insects seemed to disappear. The king reconsidered his decision, wondering if he had granted freedom to the Israelites prematurely. Once again, he took away their liberty. In that moment, the king's memory of the devastating judgments that had caused so much damage seemed to fade away.

The king shook his head in defiance, recovering from his wicked temper. He had the same angry look on his face and the same voice filled with rage. He experienced an unnerving sense of abandoning the gods of the outer world, who had caused the nation to tumble into a stupor.

Casting a fleeting glance at Moses, he barely skipped a beat. In his mind, the plague was just another one of Moses's deceptive ploys, not the work of God. Unyielding and resolute, the pharaoh refused to set them free. Day by day, fear and terror weighed on their hearts.

After this, the king was forced to face the final manifestation of the curse of death brought upon the people of Egypt.

The Israelites were commanded to sprinkle the blood of a lamb on the doorposts of their houses. Each family would take a lamb, slaughter it, and place some of the blood on the door frames of their homes. They were told to offer sacrifice and purify their house with blood smeared on their tents and at the entrances of their living quarters. None of the Israelites were to go outside until morning.

The death angel saw blood on the doorposts of the Israelites while the rest of the nation lost every firstborn, man, or beast. The death angel passed over the Israelites dwelling and turned with a vengeance on the Egyptians.

"It is the Passover sacrifice to the Lord, who passed over the houses of the Israelites in Egypt and spared our homes when he struck down the Egyptians."

The gruesome slaughter began at midnight. Between the twilight of darkness and the dawn of morning, the destroyer roamed nationwide on a campaign of death, killing the firstborn of any family who didn't have blood smeared on their doorposts on the night of the Passover.

The Lord said, "About midnight, I will go through every part of Egypt. Every oldest son in Egypt will die. The oldest son of Pharaoh, who sits on the throne, will die. The oldest son of the enslaved woman, who works at her hand mill, will die. All of the male animals that were born first to their mothers among the cattle will also die. There will be loud crying all over Egypt. It will be worse than it's ever been before. And nothing like it will ever be heard again. But among the people of Israel, not even one dog will bark at any man or animal. Then you will know that the Lord treats Egypt differently from us."

The following day, the Egyptians were stunned at the dead bodies lying everywhere and the carcasses of animals killed in the fields. Throughout the night, the death angel went house by house into pastureland, slaughtering firstborn men or beasts.

The Pharaoh, the grand vizier, and the religious leaders were all filled with grief. Nothing could explain what had happened in Egypt, and this carnage of death initiated an insane madness by a young pharaoh and his grand vizier, who was the epitome of evil in a nation that had faith in the fifth heavens and the gods of the outer world.

The Egyptians living near the king's palace protested in horror and demanded that the Israelites be allowed to leave Egypt so the nation could be freed from its misery.

With a trembling voice, the Pharaoh said to Moses, "Leave my people and go."

This decree of freedom was made before daybreak while the Egyptians looked on, some with tears of joy while others were outraged. The departure was warm, and everyone was quickly accepted with hugs and kisses.

Some elites were envious as they thought of all the free labor leaving the nation. The Israelites had paid their dues with hard labor, only to experience the faith of being treated less than human and treated like enemies of Egypt.

The citizens of Egypt brought gifts and food to the Israelites. They honored them with love since they'd become acquainted during their lifetime in Egypt, despite the fact the governance structure and religious system had used the Israelites for their benefit.

Soon, the king believed that the magic arts of Moses had outplayed him, so he went after the Israelites. It seemed that the dark side of the fifth heavens was about to go down in disgrace, but only for a short time.

In the early dawn, the pharaoh went after Moses and the Israelites with a host of his brave soldiers.

His anger had become so deep with revenge that he made a mad dash toward the trail that led out to the sea. The sudden deaths of all the firstborns of Egypt haunted the pharaoh, and he had a hunger for retaliation.

The outcome of the Tenth Plague led to a full-scale clash between the Israelites and the Egyptian military, with Horemheb on the hunt for Moses.

The young ruler dashed into the barren wasteland, his chariot racing wildly. A steep price awaited him for his unchecked frenzy as anguish soon replaced his fury. In a blink of an eye, Tutankhamun tumbled from his chariot, sustaining a grave wound and breaking both his leg and shoulders.

The young king's shoulders and lower body were severely wounded, bleeding profusely. A jagged shard of metal had sliced through his skin, leaving him critically unwell. Crimson blood oozed from his upper thigh as his eyes took on a bluish-red hue.

An eerie quiet shrouded the scene as the injured king was escorted back to the palace. His once-reliable chariot had betrayed him, subjecting him to weeks of agonizing pain.

The young pharaoh treaded wearily, striving to regain his strength and assert his authority as king. Despite his efforts, his health deteriorated under the unforgiving shadow of midnight. Fate had ensnared him in a malicious trap as his condition worsened with lethal repercussions.

Slowly, Tutankhamun's legs and feet decayed, and his moans grew more intense from the pain consuming his body. As he fought to sit up, the grand vizier, his trusted advisor, observed, while the priest murmured about the looming threat of death.

The injury was too much, but Osiris had strong, convalescing powers and weighed the hearts of the dead in the underworld. The guards rushed through the door to summon Horemheb. Everyone became silent!

As they attentively stood and listened, the High Priest's rhythmic hymns to Amun filled the air. Meanwhile, the young man's light brown eyes fluttered open and closed. The golden vessel gleamed as oil was used to cleanse his wounds. As time slowly passed, his strength diminished and the infectious disease relentlessly spread throughout his body.

As the king's feverish body struggled towards recovery, he could only await the arrival of Anubis, the death god with the head of a jackal. Chaos and conflict erupted among the soldiers, with the palace itself in disarray.

The young pharaoh's final gasps echoed through the halls, and word of the king's grave injury reached both Upper and Lower Egypt. The nation felt its effects like a punch to the gut.

Perhaps the deaths of the firstborns took the nation to a spirit of insanity. Now a young king had unexpectedly died at the age of nineteen. The nation was falling apart as the people faced uncertain possibilities.

Raphael indeed had a distaste for the greedy priests in Egypt. So did Moses. The religious leaders surrounded themselves with free labor from enslaved people, who were used to construct palaces and temples.

The elegant temples and mansions were built for noble citizens, while wages were siphoned to the priests and emperor. They gave no thought to the consequences of their evil deeds.

When the young Tutankhamun died, his chief advisor, Sage Ay, ascended to the throne. King Tut had no heir. His wife, Ankhsenamun, had no surviving children. Her threat to the throne was short-lived as the powerful grand vizier, who had a grasp on the seat of power, continued to govern.

CHAPTER 17

The Egyptian Empire was a splendid nation built by Africans. The golden age of the Egyptians expanded into a dominant imperial power, complete with pyramids, decorated burial chambers, and hieroglyphic monuments, as well as revolutionary changes in artistic renovations.

The Egyptians had completely lost touch with the Hebrews' God, as they embraced a lifestyle of joy and entertainment. They depended on trusting their high spirits to ensure success.

Even during death ceremonies, they became obedient to the gods of the afterlife and consistently disobeyed their source of blessings.

They believed the nation's health depended on faith in these abominable gods and sought after them in every way possible.

Superstition was in the air, and tradition indicated loyalty to the evildoer from generation to generation. The worship of idols was a continuous cycle.

Raphael was one of the chief guardian angels of the Tree of Life before he fell from the seventh heavens and entrance to the earthly domain.

Raphael was known to be "The Shining One Who Heals," his anointing spirit wrestled with humanity's division, but no pleading could change their hearts from corruption. In a heartfelt moment, he revealed his mortal form, but just as quickly, he was whisked away to the seventh heavens.

While in the temple, Raphael entered an intense trance before Moses' arrival in Egypt. He exclaimed, "I witnessed three impure spirits, resembling frogs, emerging from the mouths of the dragon, the beast, and the false prophets. They are demonic spirits capable of performing incredible feats."

The frogs were a method of punishment by a great plague in opposition to the message of the seventh heavens. The spirit of the fifth heavens only increased the punishment as ministers of evil came out of the mouths of false prophets.

The covenant with the gods of the outer world and a renewed spirit with death filled the air. The magicians brought forth frogs with their enchantments by the powers of the fifth heavens.

The magicians tried to bring forth lice with their enchantments but failed to do so.

The magicians said to the new Pharaoh, "This is the finger of God." Their failed enchantment did not persuade Pharaoh Ay.

They said it was the doing of God, and such attempts would be blasphemy, but Pharaoh's heart grew hard, and he didn't believe them. The magicians said nothing else as if their thoughts had disappeared.

It was enough for the magicians to become submissive and confess their powers were inferior before Moses.

Without warning, a swarm of flies entered the house of Pharaoh and became troublesome for the servants, tormenting both men and animals on the outskirts of the cities.

As simple as that, the flies appeared everywhere—some biting and nagging and bringing a mixture of diseases. The flies stung the skin, which no tonic could heal. Some of the flies harmed the body with the kiss of death.

Suddenly, the Pharaoh heard Moses's voice: "Thus saith the God of Israel: Let my people go, that they may hold a feast unto Me in the wilderness."

There was no remedy, for the plague had taken the form of a disease that infested the bodies of all the people the insects touched with loathsome sores and rashes, which bathing or ointments couldn't heal. Even as the plagues brought intense illness and death, the nation brutally worked the Israelites with heavy burdens.

The new Pharaoh, Sage Ay, was just as stubborn as King Tut. He had been the chief vizier of Akhenaten, Nefertiti, Meritaten, and Tutankhamun. Ay was no stranger to the heart of the nations, having previously served as the Master of Horses at Amenhotep III's court.

For the next four years, the sun shone brightly over the land of Egypt as the dark clouds held back the hail from the heavens. The plague of locusts, insects, and frogs had nearly vanished. The gnats and flies all died off too.

The locusts were cast suddenly into the Red Sea by a strong west wind. The venomous snakes returned to their hiding spots, and the stench of decaying creatures finally faded away.

The Israelites, led by Prince Moses, had also disappeared, heading toward the plains covered by a cloud with an appearance of fire.

The moderately aged king Ay, son of Yuya, who served as a member of the priesthood and non-Egyptian blood, had captured the throne by marrying Tutankhamun's widow, Ankhsenamun. This revolutionary change was between the new monotheistic faith and the old polytheistic religious transformation.

His reign began with the open-of-the-mouth ceremony during Tutankhamun's funeral. He wore the Blue Crown, the iconic symbol of royalty.

The new king of Egypt was accompanied by Tiye, an older wife, and his younger Great Royal wife, Ankhsenamun. The plagues followed each pharaoh as if they were a cyclical nightmare.

The younger General Horemheb was just a breath away from the throne but seemed to be walking in the shadow of Ay. His voice had been drowned out by the swift rise of his rival, Nakhtmin, a royal scribe and military commander under Tutankhamun.

Nakhtmin was a blood relative to King Ay, who paved the way for becoming the crown prince. There was still anger in the air in Egypt.

The Pharaoh said, "What have we done? We've let the people of Israel go! We've lost our slaves and all the work they used to do for us!" He stood tensely, like a drunk, still staring in the direction of the Israelites as they journeyed to freedom.

King Ay sent two hundred thousand armed soldiers after Moses as the Israelites traveled through the mountains and deserts toward the Red Sea. The mighty force chasing the Israelites intensified with six hundred chariots and fifty thousand cavalries on horseback to cut them off from any route taken into the desert.

Some of the Israelites found refuge in the crevices of mountains during the night but felt helpless and began to blame Moses for their anguish. They had no weapons.

The Egyptians followed the Israelite's every footstep. The Egyptians watched their every move, overlooking their journey from the mountains.

The Pharaoh said, "They are bewildered by the land. The wilderness has closed them in."

The Egyptians looked on as the Israelites became helpless. They turned out to be surrounded near the seashore by the Egyptian army.

Like strange waves, the awful sound of galloping horses rose from the mountains at lightning speed. The mighty Egyptian forces covered the seashore and prepared to slaughter the escaping Israelites.

The Israelites were surprised and believed they'd become victims of the pharaoh.

Their tone was sharp against Moses, saying, "Let us alone that we may serve the Egyptians. It would have been better for us to serve the Egyptians than die in the wilderness."

The noise of thunder changed everything as the soldiers lifted their heads toward the darkened sky. The galloping horse became frightened when dreadful thunder and lightning lit up the fiery sky. Thunderbolts accompanied by fiery flashes became weapons of war, as a strong easterly wind foretold potential dangers emerging from the African desert. A powerful gust swept through the Nile Delta, filling the air with a drum-like roar.

Despite this, a road appeared, dividing the sea and creating a safe pathway for the Israelites. A powerful eastern wind caused the sea to recede, leaving a passage of dry land and splitting the waters of the Yam Suf in the Nile Delta through a miraculous force.

A pillar of clouds with the brightness of flaming fire illuminated the African sky. A glowing beam of light turned darkness into daylight, yet no light benefited the Egyptian army.

Their eyes dimmed as the radiant beam of light faded. The Israelites were guided through the sea passage by a pillar of cloud during the day and a pillar of fire at night.

Meanwhile, Pharaoh observed the unfolding events while strong winds created a barrier against the waters of the Sea of Reeds, leading the Israelites out of Egypt. A powerful wind emerged, causing the sea to surge with tumultuous waves.

The surge of hissing water created a blanket of darkness over the Egyptian territory. A powerful sandstorm emerged, followed by rain showers from the heavens.

A gust of fresh air ushered in a swirling windstorm, accompanied by quivering vibrations. The calm waters created a clear path through the passage.

The Egyptians eventually gained the courage to pursue through the passageway. As the barrier transformed into a protective wall for the Israelites, it became a deadly snare for the Egyptians.

Soon, the tumultuous waves in the depths of the sea began to subside, engulfing everything in their path. The water reclaimed the horses, chariots, and all the soldiers who had pursued the Israelites into the depths.

Word of the Israelites' journey spread along the Mediterranean coast, and the natural forces in the Nile Delta offered a glimpse of an incredible cloud visible from afar, accompanying them on their long trek towards freedom.

In every city along the Nile, whispers about the miraculous escape through the wilderness filled the air. The Israelites had triumphantly broken free from Egyptian bondage and were now journeying toward Canaan, their future homeland.

The rising panic made its way up the Mediterranean coast, where many natives in the surrounding region lived under slavery and oppression by the Philistines.

Through it all, the chaos and confusion gave the natives an opportunity to rebel against Philistine rule and other forces that left the Balkans to take refuge in Canaan.

Like a giant wave, a cry of terror stirred up emotions throughout the coastal cities. The Moab citizens, whom Moses called his brothers, had as much animosity toward the Israelites as the Egyptians.

In bitterness, Moses chose to journey a longer route by traveling through the rocky hills instead of a direct way through Moab on the eastern shore of the Dead Sea.

Envy had become deeply embedded in Mediterranean society instigated by the fifth heavens, with paganism and idolatry frequently creating rifts between close relatives. One notable example involved faithless followers shaping a golden calf to worship during Moses' absence. Both gold and silver were utilized in this materialistic world to demonstrate reverence for various deities.

Confusion was in the air, and the Israelites began to move away from the Hebrew faith. They rebelled from the covenant between the Lord and the Israelites. They persuaded Aaron to take items of gold—

such as earrings and ornaments—to build a molten calf and altar to venerate a sacred cow.

The life of Moses came to an end, but the struggle for freedom carried on with Joshua reciting the passages from the Book of the Law before the gathered people of Israel.

Joshua's words resonated throughout the African sky, rallying various native tribes, including Ethiopian warriors, to protect the Israelites in their journey. The Ethiopian warriors never paused. They tirelessly supported the lengthy caravan traversing the African landscape, guiding them towards their destined home in Israel and, ultimately, to liberation.

Under Joshua's leadership, a unified force conducted a nighttime assault on the Philistines. The Lord commanded the sun to stand still and the moon's shadow to conceal daylight until the invaders residing in Israel were vanquished.

> *"And it came to pass when all the kings who were on this side of the Jordan, in the hills and the lowland and in all the coasts of the Great Sea toward Lebanon— the Hittite, the Amorite, the Canaanite, the Perizzite, the Hivite, and the Jebusite—heard about it, that they gathered together to fight with Joshua and Israel with one accord" (Joshua 9:1-2).*

BIBLIOGRAPHY

Anderson, S. (1995). The Black Holocaust For Beginners. London: Writers and Readers Publishing, Inc.

Basten, T.V. (2015). Ancient Egypt: The Egypt of Nefertiti. History Plaza.

Cartwright, M. (2016, April 8). Atlantis. Retrieved May 16, 2019, from Ancient History Encyclopedia: https://www.ancient.eu/at-Lantis/.

Catherine Leah Palmer. (2018). Akhenaten's Poem of Praise to The Sun. Retrieved 3-25, 2019, from Superstition: http://www.palmy-ria.co.uk/superstition/akhenaten.htm.

Conrad, J. (1999). Heart of Darkness. New York: Random House Publishers.

Cummins, J. (2010). The World's Bloodiest History: Massacre, Genocide, And The Scars They Left On Civilizations Beverly: Fair Winds Press.

Donnelly, I. (2008). The Atlantis: The Antediluvian World. Ellison, R. (1980). Invisible Man. New York: Random House, Inc.

Fairchild, M. (2018, August 20). Passover Feast for Christians. Retrieved April 1, 2019, from ThoughtCo.: https://www.thoughtco.Com/bible-feast-of-Passover-700185.

Flavius, J. (1998). Josephus The Complete Works. Nashville: Thomas Nelson, Inc.

Gills, J. and Nash, R. (2002). A Biblical Economics Manifesto. Lake Mary: Creation House.

Godwin, M. (1990). Angels an Endangered Species. New York: Simon And Schuster.

Greenwood, S. (2006). The Encyclopedia Of Magic Witchcraft: An illustrated historical Reference to Spiritual Worlds. London: Hermes House.

Hoope, J. (2012). The Tenth Plague and The Passover. Retrieved March 31, 2019, from BibleLessons4Kidz.com: https://bible.org/seriespage/4-tenth-plague-and-passover-exodus-11-13.

Wendi Wilkes (March 30, 2020). Coronavirus (COVID-19) and Drinking Water. https://www.asdwa.org/.

Jackson, J. G. (2001). Introduction to African Civilizations. New York: Kensington Publishing Corp.

Lumpkin, J. B. (2011). The Books of Enoch. Blountsville: fifth Estate Publishers.

Mahfouz, N. (1998). Akhenaten Dweller in Truth. New York: The American University in Cairo Press.

Millington, T. S. (n.d.). Signs and Wonders in the Land of Ham: The Ten Plagues of Egypt with Ancient and Modern Parallels and Illustrations. London: Leopold Classic Library.

Millmore, M. (2007). Imagining Egypt: A Living Portrait of the Time of the Pharaohs. New York: Black Dog & Leventhal Publishers.

Moran, M. (2007). Queen of Egypt Daughter of Eternity Nefertiti. New York: Crown Publishers.

Noss, D. S. (1999). A History of the World's Religions. Upper Saddle River: Prentice-Hall, Inc.

Oxford University. (2003). The Oxford History of Ancient Egypt. New York: Oxford University Press.

Phillips, G. (1998). Atlantis and the Ten Plagues of Egypt: The Secret History Hidden in the Valley of the Kings. Rochester: Bear & Company.

Prentice Hall. (2000). The Prentice Hall of African American Literature. Upper Saddle River: Prentice-Hall, Inc.

Reader 's Digest Association. (1981). Atlas of the Bible. Pleasantville: The Reader 's Digest Association, Inc.

Reybrouck, D. V. (2010). Congo: The Epic History of a People. New York: Harper Collons Publishers.

Shepard, A. (2017). The Atlantis dialogue. Oxford: Oxford University Press.

The Reader's Digest Association, Inc. (1978). The Word's Last Mysteries. Pleasantville: Reader's Digest.

Thomas Nelson, Inc. (1982). The Holy Bible King James Version. Nashville: Thomas Nelson Publishers.

Thomas Nelson, Inc. (1995). Nelson's New Illustrated Bible Dictionary. Nashville: Thomas Nelson Publishers.

Wells, H. G. (2017). The Invisible Man. Overland Park: Digireads.
Com Publishing.

Benson, Carmen. (1970). Supernatural Dreams and Visions. Logos
International. Plainfield.

ABOUT THE AUTHOR

Michael Ray Lemons was born in Dothan, Alabama, on September 19, 1961. He grew up and attended the public school system in Dothan and later attended Spark Technical College in Eufaula, Alabama, and Wallace Community College in Dothan. He earned three degrees in the technical field—electrical technology, computer electronics, and industrial electronics technology.

He works as a wastewater technician, a vital service during the critical coronavirus pandemic. The EPA administrator has deemed water and water treatment employees as essential workers during the public health crisis to minimize the spread of COVID-19.

The coronavirus pandemic is like the plagues sweeping the countries along the Nile at the height of the Eighteenth Dynasty.

The era of the Eighteenth Dynasty, part of the New Kingdom, is considered to have produced some of the greatest rulers who reunified Egypt under native rule. The epidemic brought Egypt, the most powerful nation in the world during this era, to its knees. Sadly, the epidemic erased much of the accomplishments of the New Kingdom. Coincidently, the coronavirus (COVID-19) pandemic happened during the writing of this novel.

ABOUT THE BOOK

This book is a fiction work with characters who folklore, classical myths, historical events, and religious works have inspired. Other parts are based on the author's imagination, who filled in the gaps left by stories open to creative adaptation. The world is filled with characters who take different shapes and forms. Whether they're angelic spirits or corporal beings, they skillfully lead men and women through their life journeys. This novel aims to explore world history, helping readers gain a deeper understanding of the connections uniting people across the globe, both spiritually and physically. Although our cultures may vary, we all share common experiences, such as living under the same sky and relying on natural elements like the wind, rain, and changing seasons. These cosmic forces bind us together, reminding us of our place in the world and our interconnectedness with one another.